Geertje Suhr

Learning About Love

A Novel

translated by Louise E. Stoehr

Culicidae Press, LLC
918 5th Street
Ames, IA 50010
USA
culicidaepress.com
editor@culicidaepress.com

Translated by Louise E. Stoehr

Images on pages 53, 72, 113 are reproductions of artwork created by Geertje Suhr. All other artwork is in the public domain.

ISBN-13: 978-1-68315-047-3

Library of Congress Control Number: 2023931035

Cover design and interior layout © 2023 by polytekton

Gorda as Isadora Duncan

I am packing: summer blouses, summer skirts, summer shoes. Because it is the summer semester, and it begins in May, and I will travel south, where the town of Tübingen is growing and beckoning more and more by the day.

But when I get there, it's raining like it was in Oldenburg, and the summer coat would better have been a winter coat. So out with the umbrella and onto shivering at the bus stop with suitcase and bag.

How is it that I'm standing here so alone? Where will I lay to rest my fears tonight? Oh, my dear book, my secure refuge, my sole friend. It's a good thing that I have my book with me.

The bus comes, and I ride it into the gray countryside. And I thought that everything in the south had already turned green. Far away from Tübingen, the bus stops in a small village: I had rented a room here while I was still in Oldenburg. The unknown room: sanctuary or trap? Scary place or homey nest?

A witch—straight out of the pages of a fairy tale—opens the door, hunched back, cane in her hand: "So, you are the student from Oldenburg, for whom I've been waiting since last evening. Finally."

The room is a bed with a narrow aisle on each side, and a tiny window, more of a hole, filled with a tree.

"Such a beautiful tree," I say. It's adorned with half-open cherry buds. So, keep looking straight outside and hold on to the buds.

Or go to bed right away.

But the old woman does not allow this: "You've got to pay upfront." The room costs forty marks, which leaves two hundred ten from the first of the month. And that will have to be enough, Dad said, that's all we have. All I have is a bed, a cherry tree in the tiny window, and a book. Oh, there's also a wardrobe in the room. Unpacking takes four and a half minutes: four and a half minutes of belongings—summer dresses and summer skirts and summer shoes.

You had thought you were traveling into summer. And I am missing my blue winter sweater, my plaid scarf, the brown gloves, the black boots, the thick wool jacket, the warm nightgown. So, to bed immediately. It's the domain of a fluffy featherbed; in some places, it bulges; in others, it crumbles to nothing. Where there's a hill, I will sweat; where there's a valley, I will have to freeze.

But better than standing in the hallway and brooding: Is this what you call living? So I plunge into sleep quickly. During the train ride at night, you just couldn't rest your eyes nor ears.

Late in the afternoon, noise from next door wakes her up. No, no noise, just the voice of the old witch and two—or three—young voices all mixed up. Quickly, Gorda puts on the summer dress and the cardigan, which is much too thin. Then there's already a knock on her door, somebody is here, and a tall woman with white hair, sternly pulled back, enters. Her two lidless and friendly doll eyes radiate down on Gorda, who sits down quickly so that there's still room in the aisle.

"I'm Marion. I'm from Vechta and also live here."

Nice, a human being, Gorda thinks. A girl friend and not just a bed, an aisle, and a cherry tree in the window hole.

They sit down in Marion's room, which is much bigger and is right next door to Gorda's room. Gorda took it for

Gorda's suitcase in Tübingen

the living area of the old woman, but it's Marion's with three respectable windows and an old stove. But the stove, unfortunately, is cold and dead. And I am cold and hungry. What are we to do?

That's when you quickly go and get mother's sandwiches. "And here, Marion, would you like one, too?" Of course, we use the formal 'you' because we are students and adults now. Marion also attends university or, rather, will attend because she hasn't been on campus yet. We can do this together.

"And I've got a warmer cardigan," Marion says. She also has a wool blanket, and that means a pair of warm feet. Right now, frozen blood is flowing from my feet up, and a cold is already taking hold in my thighs. Marion's room has a big table in the middle with five wobbly chairs. People used to eat lunch here. But the most important item is the oil heater.

"We don't have oil," Marion says. "We've got to get some right away."

The old woman knocks and, in the same instant, opens the door: "Here, I have somebody else for you to meet."

"I'm Hermione Müller," the new girl says in a stern voice and has a stern gaze for Marion and Gorda because they are sitting there in candlelight with an apple and a sandwich. "Why aren't you at university and learning?" her gaze says.

Then she goes to her room. It's off further down the hallway, off to the side, so you don't have to always fear stern gazes and words that combine reproach and threat.

"Hermione already got here a week before semester start," Marion says. "She's already been to campus, has registered, met professors, explored the town, cleaned her room, and bought textbooks and notebooks. Now she's ready to start with her studies while we trade cardigans and sandwiches and despairingly jiggle at the oil heater: Will it work?

"Of course, it works," the old woman screams, "It just needs oil, but that's not included in the paltry rent." And she slams the door shut behind her as though she had something to protect.

Starting her studies—Gorda isn't ready for that at all, neither on the inside nor on the outside. Externally, she doesn't have her textbooks, her notebooks, her winter coat, and boots. Internally, I miss my room in Oldenburg, Mother and Dad, my courage, and my girl friends. And yet, for a whole year, she has been looking forward to going to university. And anticipation is the greatest pleasure. But not the only pleasure, I hope, Gorda thinks.

Going to university—that's like a gigantic library, and you always stroll among books, take this one or that one and say: tremendous, the knowledge of this woman. Or of that man. And knowledge falls from the books into your brain. In this manner, our head becomes a gigantic library, and if someone asks you: tell me, who again was the man who renewed the empire, then you do not hesitate for long. You don't say, I've got to check that in the encyclopedia; instead, you pull the correct book from your head, where it says—as you learned and wrote with your own blood and sweat—Charlemagne! And, in this manner, you become a walking library and, when you travel, you never just simply see a castle, a palace, a castle in ruins on the Rhine River. You see Liselotte of the Palatine, as she writes letters to her aunt in Germany; she is the wife of the Sun King's brother. Like a god of war, this Sun King swept across the castles on the Rhine and Moselle rivers, because he demanded a dowry for Liselotte. But she did not want the dowry. And all that is in her letters. And now these letters are in your head. Before, they had been in the library of Tübingen on that Thursday morning in May, when you rode the bus into town to enroll in the university. You went to the library immediately so that you could recover from these strange gazes and the confusing rows of houses. You took your comfort book with you and another one about German literature. And, in this way, over the course of reading and studying for five or six years, your head is to grow into a library, just like the heads of the professors most certainly already are. You just cannot forever have to look up everything first.

There's now a fourth female student living with us. I didn't even know that there was still another little room on our floor. Two male students live on the floor above us. I don't know how the old woman lives. She always slams the door shut behind her as though she had something to protect. The fourth young woman in our band of students is called Susette, sports red bouffant curls and a great deal of artificial face on her face. Even her over-sophisticated fingernails cry out for a calling other than the daily fingering of books. These kinds of hands want to finger elsewhere. Pudgy, they always hold a cigarette at a slant.

"Why don't you stop smoking for a while," Hermione says sternly. "It gives me asthma."

But Susette, whose actual name is Susie, firmly points her index finger at the door at the back of the hallway: "Why don't you go jump in a lake."

Hermione's lake is strictly focused on her studies. Her books are lined up in two rows on the desk against the wall, where she calculates, traces with a compass, and draws ellipses. Hermione has all the torture instruments of mathematics in her toolbox. She plans on applying them to math-deficient high-school girls: here I'll nip your silliness with algebra, and there I'll rip out your fancy ideas with integrals. And that's the figure Hermione cuts herself: no silliness and no fancy ideas. Those thoughts have been dispelled by her love for mathematics. That's the way in which true love dispels all other love. Like the one for heavy make-up and bows.

Of those, Susette owns a bunch. Bows hang from her ponytails, bows adorn her collar, and bows are attached to her waist.

"Tell me, why did you bring so many clothes," Marion asks with genuine interest as she peeks into Susette's room. There's a whole fashion boutique hanging from the curtain rod because the wardrobe—which happens to be the largest one in the entire house—is too small. The hunchbacked old woman magically had assigned each one of us to the appropriate room.

Wand waved high—and Gorda goes there: she loves mainly her bed and a book. She does not need more than an aisle around the bed and a tiny window like a hole—covered with a cherry tree, and she's set for the merry life of a student.

And Hermione goes here: above all, she needs a desk along the wall for books with numbers, a case for compasses, and no distracting view of the orchard. It is always at her back—no eyes and no ears—where it can do no harm with its tempting calls: "Oh, just come on out here!"

And Susette has the gigantic wardrobe in which all their clothes could fit if she hadn't imported an entire fashion boutique from Passau.

And Marion gets the largest room with an oil heater, which is now radiating its oily warmth, so when it becomes too cold for the others in their cubbyholes—they probably once were storage rooms and not real rooms, Gorda thinks—then they all sit on wobbly chairs around Marion's big table. Marion's room is the only one with such an abundance of chairs. And Marion always has sandwiches, and cookies, and chocolate, and wine, and she hands out cardigans and blankets to those who are really freezing. Three candles shine their light on the chewing mouths of the studying girls. In this way, it is almost fun to be a student.

The first lecture class: It takes place in an amphitheater. Tübingen has thousands of students, and they all must be able to hear that knowledge somewhere, so the old Greek and Roman tendency for much round space seems to be just right.

At the very top, in the last row—that's where I sit down. That way I have a view from above at a distance of what's to come.

And what comes into the room ... is not a Roman emperor. This one walks with a slight slouch, a forehead like a full moon on top of a mind-consumed lanky frame. He obviously carries the heavy load of his head-library, and under his arm he holds two more splendid books. The little man—is he really that small, or is he dwarfed by perspectival foreshortening?—fumbles with a microphone. It crackles and clanks in the lecture hall. "Silence, please," someone shouts. The students rustle with their last notebook pages. Next to me, a girl is eating something. I'm also eating: I'm eating up the professor's words. Never before have I heard a professor lecture: He reads aloud from a book—his book.

"He wrote that already ten years ago," my neighbor states arrogantly. As if he himself had written three books in the meantime. I write down what I hear. In front of me several students are talking with each other. "When are you coming—I can't on Tuesday—tomorrow, I've got to ..." Bits of sentences like these puncture the literary texture on my notebook page. For that reason, it remains three quarters blank. I place a fat line under the title of the book being read: That's what's important here. I order it in the nearest bookstore.

"What? You don't even have the book by Professor Hitzig in stock?"

"Now listen!" The young bookstore clerk calls out, combat-ready. "You're not the first one to be here. You're just number four hundred twenty or so."

Hurt, number four hundred twenty or so walks to the bus. I didn't know that I am a number. And for the professor, I'm not even a number: I am a point—all the way up there at the edge of the amphitheater.

An unnoticed dot. You have to fight hard so that the dot turns into a dot-dot, into comma and dash, into a face, into a person—but five hundred fellow dots are also fighting for a face. And is the whole thing even worth it?

We actually live in the country. Together with Marion, I take a walk through the forest when the May sun finally shines. An advance guard of leaves sticks its tip of the nose into the air:

Is it clear? can we come? But it's pouring rain again the next day. The oil heater glows to the brim, candles are lit, cookies handed out, and we celebrate Christmas in May. Such a small and miserable Christmas feast. But it's better than going to bed or sitting on the edge of the bed.

Tübingen has narrow streets and little houses and little squares full of students. A gigantic current of bodies crosses the small town. This current surges out of windows, it bursts into confectioneries, it meanders through shops, it strolls across meadows. You just can't read and learn all the time—that's what's written all over their faces. The final exams are still an unfathomable distance away: All the beautiful things, however, are so close by. Along the riverbanks, the first-semester students lazily lounge about and patiently wait for their knowledge to grow. Where the more advanced students lounge about, I don't know—probably in their rooms, like Hermione, who's already studying for her exam in five years.

"Anticipatory studying is the best studying," her narrow lips warn.

The third lecture class: With full force, May bursts through the mighty windows of the amphitheater. The little man in front—why do all professors seem so bowed down with knowledge?—reads mutteringly. I take notes and I don't. In a week, I'll get his book, the young bookstore clerk promised, then I'll catch up and read ahead.

How truly beautiful May is! Everywhere it gnaws gaps into the rows of the studying, writing, and chewing figures. We've already won a quarter of the seats. You could lie down here or there if you wanted to, but you don't want to, after all: We're here to learn and not to sleep. Oh, how truly beautiful May is!

The students who live on the floor above us, Jörg and Stefan, only sleep here and study all day in town, or what do they do there? But in the evening, they drink wine with us and hold their hands to the oil heater when the next-to-last winter wind of May howls about the house. And they bring their ration of cookies and candles, and you move closer together like family because you're so alone and far away from home and because you need comfort, each other, and sun.

When the professor doesn't read from his own book, then he reads from someone else's, and then you buy someone else's; and when he reads from the loose notes of a book he's working on, then you can still find some book on this topic. For example, there are hundreds of books about Eichendorff. Why am I sitting here if there are books about Eichendorff, which I can read much easier at home?

May advances and turns into June. June's sun finally forces green into May's forests and turns colorful students into walking primroses. The amphitheaters stand half-empty when the sky is cloudy, and three-quarters empty when the sky is blue. And suddenly they fill up with umbrellas, notebooks, and sandwiches—and you try to find a seat in vain.

In the town, there's a confusing hustle and bustle: Are they here to pursue their studies or to get to know each other? Susette spends hours in Café Weiting. You meet the best guys there, she says.

Every day, I wave at her on my way to the amphitheater. I guess, she never has class at that time. She's also not lugging books around as the others are. Even those who are lounging about the river always have a book with them. As headrest or decoration for the meadow. Or are these bologna sandwiches by any chance?

Dad had used his connections, and Gorda received an invitation—to the grand summer party. Now you have to go through all your summer things, which you had unpacked in four-and-a-half minutes. Dear God, I only have no sensible clothes—well-behaved and sensible just won't be appropriate. Marion, can you help me? But Marion brought, in addition to winter jackets and winter blankets, only clothes appropriate for class. It's no use, you've got to knock on Susette's door.

"Oh, I see," Susette says, "Do come in, and help yourself."

Susette has no clothes appropriate for class; Susette has only clothes appropriate for fun. In red, pale yellow, white with blue polka dots, black-green. I take the three dresses without irritating bows and stand in my aisle around the bed. Susette is much rounder up here than I am, also here and there on the sides, but I am taller. And what Susette fills out in chest and waist, I fill with height. Yet, a wonder: what shouldn't fit, does. Where do we have a mirror? It is—totally misplaced—in Hermione's wardrobe. Hermione is studying in town at this time, so you enter her room without knocking. Susette does this whenever Hermione goes strolling along on her mathematics jaunts. In the sliver of a mirror—regrettably, the mirror ended up too narrow—Gorda sees a stick with big blue polka dots. And that's what I've been dieting for, just to tower like a stick. No, let's get the stick dress off and the red one on. It fits snuggly and bulges where there's little, yet something that does bulge. This way, even a stick is rounded out to a desirable figure.

"You do have a beautiful figure," Susette says annoyed. "I definitely have to quit eating those chocolate-coated marshmallow puffs. I already look like one!" And angrily, she hits her pretty behind with her cupped hand. Gorda would like to have such a behind.

On the day of the party, the student who was arranged to be her escort comes to pick her up. In America, this is called a *blind date*. The more blind, the more sight with which you look at the other person. You downright stare at his broad-domed forehead, the pimples on the sides of his cheeks and on his forehead. And he stares back with a look that asks: How am I going to survive this evening? So, you immediately forget his pimples and think about your own mouth, heart-shaped and way too small. And your stern chin and your eyes, which radiate like the south only because of mascara. This way, all things balance out.

<hr>

In the fraternity house, the lower rooms are full of chairs and tables at which couples who are strangers sit and ogle each other. Those who laugh and make a racket have known each other for a long time.

Oh, if only I'd known Heinrich for a long time. And he'd open his wide and spongy mouth and speak in the most delicate sentences of Eichendorff and Rilke. But Heinrich is majoring in economics, and I can't make out a single word of it.

"Heinrich, explain to me why one studies economics." And Heinrich explains and guzzles beer after beer while I sip my wine and warn myself: Careful, you had hardly anything to eat; that little bit of bread and butter won't keep you full for long. I wish I'd bought chicken breast—"Economics is an incredibly interesting field," Heinrich says—but money is so tight, and you do want to go to the opera with Marion and Susette—"and it is debatable whether economics of business administration is the right field," Heinrich says—and every bus ride into town costs one mark, which is a lot for the little bit of money I have left to spend—"and for this reason, I finally landed on economics," Heinrich says—I also skimp on food to save money for books; I skimp on food for all nice things—"even though my father is a teacher and wants me to become a lawyer," Heinrich says.

"I've got to eat something, or I'll faint," Gorda says with such fervor as though she had to prove it. And, puzzled, Heinrich jumps up with a hand motion: I don't want any proof here, and he disappears into the back rooms. That's where they must have sandwiches with butter and cheese, ham, or bologna. Everywhere, students are balancing these sandwiches on their way through the room.

This way, you can sit and can look around.

Without the arranged Heinrich. Instantly, the gnaw of the hunger saw stops nagging. Maybe, it wasn't hunger, after all. But the sandwiches fill a great void in heart and stomach, so you can order another glass of wine and murmur (you like to speak with your mouth full), "Heinrich, do you have siblings?" And Heinrich actually does have siblings. And now the music starts and overwhelms Heinrich's other siblings. And so you dance. Dancing is conversation without words, calmness within noise. And it's only during the pauses that you keep asking: "So, Heinrich, what do you plan on doing after you graduate?" Fearlessly, Heinrich drones on. I'm at home here, his sentences say. This is my fraternity. This is where they drink together in the evenings. Like dancing, drinking connects people without words. All the male students here are his drinking buddies. And Gorda's only friends are the wine, the dinner rolls, and the arranged Heinrich. No wonder that Heinrich is happier to eat, drink, and talk than she is. Often, he also stands at the bar with his day-by-day and night-by-night companions and reports on something.

He's hopefully not giving them reports about me?

"Heinrich, I've got to catch the 11 o'clock bus. The next one will leave at six in the morning, so I'd rather leave now."

Heinrich's mood instantly changes: from arranged to self-determined. He puts his arm around Gorda's red Susette-shoulder.

"Now, now, not so fast, young lady. First, we'll drink and pledge friendship."

A third glass of wine easily achieves the change from formal to informal "you," and his kiss is planted on her less sensitive cheek because she turns her mouth away.

More and more couples disappear into the garden as though there was dancing going on there, too.

"What are they doing there?" Gorda asks.

"Oh, they show the tower to the girls," Heinrich says.

"What tower?"

"We have an observation tower in our garden, a relic from old wartimes. And when it gets light in the morning, I'll show you the tower."

Now Gorda waits for the tower, but actually for the bus. Anticipation is always the greatest pleasure. Finally, light from outside radiates on the few remaining dancers.

The light shifts contours and emaciates the skin. Within a few minutes, beauties of the night pale to shades of Hades.

"My god, you've got a great tan," Heinrich says surprised.

So it has paid off to lie on the meadow in front of our house, the Eichendorff book under your head or on your stomach, and sometimes you actually open it up—but now someone is talking about something again.

"Now I'll show you the tower," Heinrich says with glistening pimples.

"But first let's go into the garden," Gorda says. And there are couples standing behind every bush and hedge. Oh, what are they doing there? Quickly, you turn around and onward to the tower. It can't be worse. You've got to go up steep stairs. Happily chuckling couples are coming down the stairs, so you step aside until they have passed. But finally, you are at the top, and unfortunately, the last couple leaves, so you are alone. Gorda makes a beeline to the edge, an image from Eichendorff rushes up to her: bright meadows on hill after hill and the fir forest behind them like a dark ruff. Well, are we in the country? I thought we were in Tübingen.

"How beautiful," Gorda says, "how calm."

At this instant, a soft bag falls against her from behind. She bends dangerously over, flailing her arms.

"Ouch!" Heinrich yells. "Watch what you're doing!"

"What are you doing?" Gorda cries out in outrage. "Are you trying to throw me down the tower?"

"I just wanted to surprise you …"

Oh, the idiot wanted to kiss me from behind.

"I want to go to the bus right now," Gorda says and hurries down the stairs.

———

At the bus stop, Heinrich says: "You're not my type anyway. The blonde who sat at the table to the left of us, you remember, she wore a white dress—she's my type.

And Gorda remembers her mouth, heart-shaped and way too small; her stern chin; and her eyes, which radiate like the south only because of mascara.

But still, I don't have to kiss just anybody, she decides.

You were allowed to buy a lottery ticket, and you drew a blank. But you never buy tickets often enough. You usually don't notice that Jörg and Stefan are men. Or you don't want to notice. After all, you already share table and edge of the bed with them. The old woman slams the door shut behind her as though she had something to protect, but she's not giving us the reproachful looks of parents, just the outraged looks of an owner: Don't you dare break my chairs. But they have been broken for a long time. She's waiting for the semester break; then she will be able to sit again at our table and sleep in our beds.

Tuesday evening, Susette comes home from her studies in the café and says: "Girls, I saw a notice on a bulletin board at the university: Looking for female dancers for American soldiers stationed here. Wouldn't that be fun?"

"Oh, no! Never any soldiers," Marion says. "They have such a bad reputation."

Hermione has a strange look like a problem from integral calculus that has no solution. American soldiers, that's Americans like all others, straight out of high school, Gorda thinks. That would be fun—I could practice my American English. Perhaps, she will draw the winning ticket, and her American is directly from California. But it turns out that he is from Minnesota.

He still has a buzz cut, a snub nose, and his American English sounds just like her Californian English. He's delighted: "Wow, you were an exchange student in California?"

This is not the way it was with the arranged Heinrich: You can talk a lot about the U.S., how things were at her school and at his. You keep talking even while dancing. While dancing or standing, while eating or drinking.

And when he takes her to the bus stop, he gets a kiss in the right place.

He will call, won't he, Gorda thinks while French sentences bang against her tired ears in the amphitheater. You've got to write down those sentences. Gorda has already filled three notebooks, but if you understood correctly, you don't know because nobody interrupts the linguistic rapid fire with the often-needed sentence: "Excuse me, would you please repeat that?" You sit there and quickly look to your left and right. Everybody takes notes as if knowing and understanding. It's only she who does not understand. If she changed over to the English hall, she'd understand just as well as these students here. In any event, I need one year in France or maybe two or three because each year of adulthood greatly shrinks the door to your brain, Max said. And Max had spent only half a year in Lausanne in the French-speaking part and now he speaks as though he was born and raised there. Max, her much admired brother: In his brain, he has the entire card catalogue that should also be in Gorda's and Heiner's—but as the first born, he snatched it all up. All that remained for Gorda and Heiner was effort. And Heiner doesn't even love effort: You can have that, Gorda; I don't want it. And so, Gorda has effort for three, all the effort and all the hard work. Shouldn't she change over to the English hall? But no, that would be too easy. What I'm already able to do, I don't have to learn. And French, that is the most ancient culture. After Latin culture came French culture. All of Europe spoke French—everywhere there were courts, and the noble knights traveled from country to country on their French sentences, which were welcome everywhere. And so Gorda wants to travel from country to country: And her English and her French will be welcome everywhere. Having two language horses pulling your wagon is better than having one. And whatever Max can do, I must learn it too, even with effort and hard work.

Then the American soldier calls, the boy from Minnesota.

"Yuck—a soldier," Marion says.

"A soldier is a human being, too," Gorda says. His name is Jack, and he asks: "Do you want to get together next Saturday?"

Of course, Gorda wants to practice her American English: "Susette, would you please lend me a dress again?"

"You don't need a going-out dress for an American soldier," Marion opines. "He's going to be just in his Army fatigues."

But Gorda decides on Susette's black-green dress because going out is going out. And the next Saturday, the doorbell rings. But it's not Jack in Army fatigues standing outside; instead, it's a classy dress uniform with a few stripes on the shoulder and wrinkles all over the face from giving orders. "Where's Jack?" Gorda asks full of hope.

"He couldn't make it," says the classy dress uniform. "I'm standing in for him tonight."

This is followed by a forced smile, and Gorda works hard at not saying: That's got to be a joke.

"No, I'm not going without Jack," Gorda says, and at this moment, a hand accustomed to give orders grabs her and drags her to the car. Oh god, he's got one of these gigantic American cars. Well, it would be fun to ride in this car... And she gets in. You just can't say "no" like that. And, maybe, he'll tell her why Jack couldn't make it.

"I'm Dick," the replacement soldier says—but he isn't a soldier, he's already got a rank—"and we're going to the movies now."

In the movie theater, he puts his arm around Susette's dress, and Gorda wishes that it would be Susette's shoulder, too. This man could be my uncle. Then Dick strokes her neck—the stiffened Gorda-neck that had been kissed by Heinrich. That's the one thing that won't happen: I won't kiss a strange uncle in a strange movie. I've got to get out of here.

"I'm getting sick," and Gorda bolts to the restroom and then to the exit. Dick, who's used to issuing orders, is already standing there and says: "We're going to a bar now."

But Gorda doesn't want to go to any bar: "I've got to go home, to bed. I'm getting a sore throat."

Indignantly, Dick throws open the car door for her lie: "Please, get in."

During the drive back, he doesn't say a word; she doesn't say a word. You stupid cow, his silences says. I know, says hers.

The next day, Jack calls. "Where were you last night?" Gorda exclaims relieved.

"I can't go out with you. My commanding officer won't allow it."

"Why not allow it?"

"I don't know either."

"His name isn't Dick by any chance?"

"How come you know his name?"

"No reason," Gorda says. "I just heard it somewhere."

So, whenever the classy dress uniform calls, she isn't home.

"You see," Marion says, "soldiers just aren't human beings; soldiers are soldiers."

How beautiful July turns out to be!

And it's ravenous; greedy, it decimates the ranks of students. The amphitheaters are getting emptier by the day. You could sit as a small group in a circle around the professor. Instead, we sit widely scattered like remote villages: Avoid all contact, that's what this means. All the while, we long from one village to the other. Over there, for instance, there is a divine guy, blond, with shoulders of an athlete, not of a thinker—what is he doing here among all the bodies that have been weakened by the mind? Why isn't he, like the others, strolling through the pleasures of forest and meadows or through the jammed narrow streets of Tübingen?

Those still studying here, that's the aspiring vanguard, the front of knowledge, the professors of tomorrow. Those who don't rove far afield today—on a beautifully balanced cool-hot and silky-blue summer midday—are born for greatness, for fifty years of turning word-soaked pages in gloriously furnished libraries that are housed in old castles or modern high-rises. Wherever they are, it is the realm of the silence of concentrated brooding, which compels a certain look on the pale, sun-shy faces, a kind of steely-fragile look.

Or is it just the many glasses that give you this look?

I sit here like a spy in enemy territory.

No dress appropriate for studying is of help here. My tan—it screams betrayal.

One afternoon, you return to the old woman's house: How beautiful July turns out to be! But inside the house, the cool night reigns—a bit too cool, a bit too much night.

"Just open the shutters, Marion."

"Do it yourself," Marion says.

Gorda walks over to the window: "Well, what's going on here? There's a scaffold in front of the window, no, around the whole house. Why didn't I notice it when I came home?"

The old woman is having the house painted, and we are sitting in the dark. Jörg and Stefan climb around the boards of the scaffold and enter our room through the window. We no longer live in a house but in a cave. During the day, you can't bear it here: We camp on the scaffold in the sun, or we go to the nearby meadows or straight away into the forest. Even Hermione is compelled into the joys of summer, but always with numbers in hand and compass in her pocket. "Just be quiet," Hermione says. "I'm in the middle of a calculation." Marion talks about her Peter, and Gorda is resting her head on a blanket.

I'm lying here, holding my head toward the sunshine instead of holding my head in a book. And yet there was nothing more I wanted to do than go to university and study, shove book after book into my brain for eternal memory, and now I am relaxing here instead of hurrying to the amphitheaters, where at least the spoken word reigns supreme. But when I'm there, I always ask myself: Why are this man's words so unclear despite microphone and pages of notes? In my notebook, I stumble over deaf gaps, so I'd rather go home and open the book that clearly says in print when and how Eichendorff lived and wrote. For me, the eyes are the door to the mind; in contrast, my ears open and close all by themselves like swaying fins in the stream of words.

But no sooner do I want to open my book on the meadow than the sun rips it away from me. Now it's lying next to me again on the blanket that Marion brought along, and my hand fingers the knowledge made of paper. If my hand were capable of reading, I'd be reading. Another lost day.

Day after day, the same battle for the book in the sun. Do I stand firm and study or do I let it be ripped from my hands? Usually, the sun wins. I still have enough time until this evening. In the evening, however, Marion and Susette get the cookies and the wine from the shelf, and the candles shine so sunlike in our house-cave, and Jörg and Stefan want to be men and be noticed, too. So you take notice of them while you pour wine into your almost empty stomach because by no means do you want to gain weight and you can use the food money for more beautiful things anyway.

At two o'clock in the morning, Gorda starts throwing up, followed by a gagging attack every half hour, then every hour—until she falls into a sleep of desperation.

"How could you possibly drink so much on an empty stomach?" Marion says at three in the morning. "Don't you ever eat real food?"

But half an hour later, she throws up, too. Even Jörg and Stefan stay in bed the next day, hung over. Everyone skimps on food and wine.

"That tastes like acid," Hermione says and retreats to her sober numbers. All the skimping also has a good side: they bought tickets for the *Flying Dutchman* in Stuttgart. Susette knows a medical student who will take us with him in his car.

On the way to the opera, Gorda already feels the pain on the left side above her eye. Like a biting rat in her brain. She takes two pain pills.

"Do you have any stronger stuff for Gorda?" Susette asks the medical student. But he hasn't got anything on him. The rat effortlessly eats the two pain pills. So she takes another two because she doesn't have anything else. The rat apparently loves these pain pills; they make it really active. Gorda closes her eyes. But how do I close my ears? If only Marion would finally stop talking about Peter. The car groans and squeaks. Susette giggles whenever the medical student says anything. This piercingly high giggle. That makes the rat really active. "Would you just stop giggling," Gorda finally says, or is it the rat in her. Susette shrieks: "I laugh whenever I want to." This means two more pain pills. The rat eats them up too and without any sign of getting tired. "She can't take anymore pills," the medical student says. If only he'd keep his mouth shut! Susette giggles again. The rat also giggles. It bites and giggles.

"Everybody—just stay quiet!" The scream came from Gorda, but it wasn't Gorda. And yet it was somebody: after all, everyone holds their tongue.

Now they all noticed that I am no longer myself. I am a rat.

"You just can't simply stay in the car," Marion says.

"I'm not going to any opera," Gorda says.

The shrieking they call singing. The rattling and tooting, the jingling and squeaking—I won't be able to stand it.

And my rat is on a rampage.

Gorda stays in the car by herself. "Please, please, go to the opera and let me stay here," she pleaded with them. The medical student wants to stay with her.

"Me too," Susette giggles.

"No, no, just go," Gorda moans. Soon she will yell: "Just go!"

But then they finally went. From then on, Gorda has lived with a rat in her brain. At times, it sleeps for a whole week, and you think that it's dead. But then in the evening, after a glass of wine with a piece of bread and an apple, you feel the scraping on the left side above your eye or on the right side above your eye or on the left side in the back of your neck. Her rat is a common rat that wanders. Sometimes, it comes from the south and stomps northward; at other times, it crisscrosses as if without destination. But it always presses strongly on this or that eye.

"I'm going blind," Gorda calls out, closes the curtain, and pulls the pillow over her eyes—this way you no longer have eyes. As compensation, your ears become giant funnels: they listen to the universe. The sound of a pencil falling is like the crash of a spruce in the forest.

Marion whispers: "Are you ill again?" And her whisper swells up to a screech.

The old woman slams the door shut behind her as though she had something to hide, and thunder rolls through your veins. Gorda presses the pillow into her ears: go away, world. Now there is only me and the rat. And, eventually, only the rat.

Reiner, the medical student, now calls Gorda and no longer Susette on the phone. "How's the rat doing," he asks. Or: "Is the rat paying you a visit again?" He brings strong medication and sits next to the bed when Gorda wants solitude. Susette turns into the rat when he leaves. While he is there, she sits by him like an angel. "Oh, Reiner, it's so kind of you to take care of Gorda. You're a regular Dr. Schweitzer!" And then she giggles. This piercingly high giggle. And when he leaves, she says: "Well, Gorda, that's the difference between you and me. I don't talk about my suffering; I endure my headaches in silence. But you have to make everything into a production." There is, however, only one production by one rat. I do not even exist here.

Until the next day. Then Gorda would have liked to borrow Susette's black-green fun dress for an evening with Reiner. But Susette isn't lending clothes anymore. "One has to think about oneself," Susette says. "And last time, you got a stain on my dress."

"But I specifically had it dry cleaned," Gorda says.

"Yes, exactly," Susette says. "I had to do without it for days."

So Gorda wears a school dress when she goes out with Reiner. He doesn't even look at it and talks only about his anatomy class. Eichendorff bores him.

"How can you possible study such silly stuff?" Reiner says. "I've always hated poems. Thank God, I chose something more tangible."

Gorda doesn't want to hear how he cuts open corpses, hey Reiner, I can't even get one bite down.

"You've got to stay objective," Reiner says. "Sentimentalism has no place in medicine."

Gorda feels woozy: that guy and I have nothing in common. Just her rat and his pills.

"You need more vitamins," he says when she tells him about her persistent tiredness. "Tell me, what do you actually eat?" When he prescribes pills for her, his gaze becomes caring. It cheers him up when she feels sick.

With him, I could talk for hours about the aches in my stomach or my throat or my shoulder. When the other say: "Oh, just stop your whining," then Reiner says: "Show me your tongue." He practices superiority. Poems crumble to pieces alongside his stethoscope. His touching hands, his listening ears. "Does it hurt here too?" he asks in a motherly tone. But if I appear in the afternoon's dress of health and talk about French, he declares in a fatherly voice: "One language is quite enough."

With him, I would have to be always veiled in suffering. In order to calm Reiner, I am sick a lot. I lie in bed with the book on Eichendorff and the French book. I haven't been to the amphitheater for weeks now. *Perhaps, you missed something,* a voice says from above my eye on the left, right where the rat lives. *The professor lectures about significant things, and you read about insignificant ones.* But this book tells me exactly when and how Eichendorff ... *Perhaps you should have attended the lectures after all,* says the voice up there on the left side. Now concentrate on this page here. *If you continue like this, you'll never graduate,* says the voice up there on the left side, where a couple of feet start scratching—or is it just my nerves. But nothing can be better than an Eichendorff biography like this one here, I counter. *You don't go to university so that you lie in bed and read,* says the voice up there on the left side, and a peculiar weight expands above my eye. My God, I think, it's the rat. *Reading—you could do that at home in Oldenburg,* says the voice up there on the left side. *You wouldn't have had to come to Tübingen to do that.* The-rat-scratches-the-rat-gnaws.

"Reiner," Gorda says on the phone, "come here immediately. I don't have any more pills." *You'll never amount to anything,* says the voice up there on the left side, *nothing at all.* "Marion, would you close the curtains. Where did my ear plugs go?" *Nothing for all eternity. Nothing, nothing at all,* says the voice.

Pillow over my eyes. My ears closed. Go away, evil world.

Nothing, nothing, says the voice.

So it's back to the amphitheaters. It's clearly a summer lull there. Have the students already gone home, or are the sitting in the numerous cafés or at the bank of the river or at the surrounding meadows? They don't have a rat in their heads.

Wherever they are: they calmly laugh, read, and eat in the streets, in the rooms, and on the meadows. The professor mumbles into the microphone. This is the next-to-last lecture. I'd better move closer to the front; I don't understand anything here. I take notes wherever I can. *Now you've missed four lectures,* says the voice up there on the left side. I write as much as I can. The Eichendorff book lies next to me: Whatever I don't understand, I will read up on. Was this eighteen-hundred-sixteen or –sixty? *What's the use of this*, says the voice up there on the left side. *It's too late anyway.* So it's a happy day when you finally start packing. Just getting away from this voice, this rat, this town.

"I'll give you a ride as far as Koblenz," Reiner says.

Gorda wants to go to Bonn to Cornelia, her girlfriend from school, who has invited her.

Reiner drives up on Thursday. The possessions of four-and-a-half minutes have long been packed into the brown leather suitcase. I knock on the old woman's door. She opens the door and forgets to close it as though she had nothing to protect.

"You want to pay," she says with a raspy voice, angrily out of habit, and for the first time I walk behind her. So this is where she has lived and waited for our departure every day: a kitchen stove and, behind it, a gurney—no, a cot—crowded by trash. She sleeps in the midst of her garbage although she dusts our rooms, which left no energy for her kitchen. Get lost, her evil looks say: What's my filth to you? Soon it will say in the *North-German City Gazette*: clean rooms for rent at affordable rates in a pretty village near Tübingen, convenient bus connections. And some Liesel or some Heike will write to Mrs. Bankert in the pretty village near Tübingen that she would like to rent the advertised room. And then you move into an unheated hole of a room in cold and rainy weather and cry your eyes out, wishing to be home. But that's called growing up: persevering by candle light, wine, and notebooks with badly taken notes—and not doubting the meaningfulness of your course of study. Really, Mom, I'm doing fine here; I just should've brought the blue sweater and my boots—and, well, a blanket maybe. Now, next time I know how to do everything better. Marion and I have rented a room together for the winter semester. It's in the middle of Tübingen and saves us the tedious bus ride. So, come winter, I will take my studies seriously. You're just not able to concentrate in the summertime anyway.

———

When they get to the Rhine, Reiner's car breaks down. Thank God, it's just the tire. But the garage is closed until two o'clock. I call Cornelia: "Hey, I won't make it to Bonn before seven o'clock."

"That's fine," Cornelia says. "I have a treat for you; you'll be surprised."

Gorda takes out a mirror: "I'm too dirty for surprises."

"Oh, quit that nonsense," Cornelia says. "We'll have a great evening." Gorda rips open the suitcase with the school clothes and looks for a clean blouse. She puts it on in the restroom at the train station. Lipstick and eyebrows have to be right, even if nothing else is right. Reiner demands a goodbye kiss: "I haven't given you a ride this far for nothing." The kiss smudges the blouse and extinguishes the gleaming lips. If only I'd changed later in the train.

"Reiner, don't. We've always been just good friends." Up there on the left side, a pressure begins. "Reiner, do you have a few pills for me?"

"I've always been good enough for that," Reiner says, and his hand moves up her blouse.

34

I'd rather have a rat in my head than a rat on my chest, Gorda thinks. But she doesn't say a thing: she is too well-mannered to do that. She even waves goodbye from the window, and then she again rips open the brown suitcase. The white blouse is no good anymore. But here is the blue-checkered blouse; in an emergency, it will ward off a surprise.

At the train station, Cornelia winks with her cheerful half-moon eyes. Gorda has an exacting look for her friend, as well as for the people to the left and right of her friend. There's no surprise here, thank goodness, Gorda thinks. Today I can do without one.

"Come on, we've got to go to the waiting area," Cornelia says. So, that's where the unwanted surprise is waiting after all. The surprise: there's two big and solid men, one of them has dark hair, bushy eyebrows like a tomcat, and a small mouth—

Outside the Bonn railroad station

or is he just pulling in his lips in such an odd way?—and the other one has blond hair, roughed-up thick lips, and the tip of his nose is crisply curved upward. As they greet her, she sees two broadly laughing mouths.

Gorda laughs, too. What else is there to do?

"Let me introduce you to Remo and his friend Peter, who is visiting. So, we can go out as a foursome."

Gorda laughs as though she likes the idea of going out as a foursome.

She has already heard about Remo. He is Swiss and rents a room from the same people as Cornelia does. His friend's got to be also Swiss. He speaks a thick dialect. Remo, in contrast, speaks standard German with recognizably correct intonation and a warmly rolling 'R', which is common on the German theater stage. The blond man quickly stows Gorda's suitcase away in the VW when Cornelia suggests an Italian restaurant. Really nearby. In the restaurant, Gorda immediately goes to the ladies' room: she hadn't expected this kind of surprise. If only I had one of Susette's fun dresses with me.

The mirror shows the truth of her narrow cheeks, her small mouth, her hair hanging down like a rag. The only way to remedy this is a glass of wine.

"My God, Gorda, you've got to be thirsty. We just took a sip of our wine, and you already finished your whole glass."

Now she blushes—but on the inside, please. She won't show anything on the outside, and she resolves to drink more slowly and to eat more slowly. Didn't Marion always tell her: "You always eat so greedily"? But it isn't greedily. It is impatiently, as impatiently as she takes notes in the amphitheater, as impatiently as she washes her hair, cleans her room, or packs her suitcase. Everything that's not reading—she does impatiently. It's a bad sign, Gorda thinks, because who can always read, lie in the sun, and talk with girlfriends?

"Gorda, now you're suddenly eating like a snail, and a little earlier you couldn't eat fast enough. Hurry up, and we'll have a glass of wine at my place."

"Remo is studying German language and literature in Bonn, where his brother is a professor in the same field. It seems that Remo wants to be like his brother," Cornelia says. "But his professor-brother is quite different: at any social gathering, he monopolizes all strands of conversation, and Remo just sits there in silence or giggles in agreement. Yes, really, Gorda, he giggles."

"I just can't image this with such a masculine man, Cornelia. He doesn't giggle, he laughs."

When Remo is relaxed, his lips are full and rosy, but when he's angry at something—he seems to be angry a lot, Gorda thinks—then his two tomcat eyebrows tighten into one bushy beam, and his lips are puckered or small. And when he laughs, only the lower part of his face looks amused, the upper part continues to be angry. It's only after many glasses of wine that the lower and upper parts laugh at the same time. There's a rupture that runs through Remo—from left to right across his face just under the tip of his nose. Peter, in contrast, laughs with ease and without fissures or cracks. And he talks a lot in his dialect, which he considers to be standard German, and which indeed contains standard German, although at times he lapses into a language that barely seems to have any connection to German.

"Are they speaking Swedish?" Gorda asks.

"Of course not," Cornelia says. "That's real Swiss German. A regular German speaker just doesn't understand it anymore."

The next day, the four of them take a stroll along the Rhine. The sky radiates warmth and well-being. "When angels travel," Cornelia says. But Gorda is no angel: she observes Remo surreptitiously. Even when she is looking at the water and at the green wine leaves, she is observing Remo. How long he speaks with Cornelia, how he then walks over to Peter and then to her, and how he stays with her for a long time. Twenty minutes, for sure. Then Cornelia comes over and takes Remo by his arm as though he belonged to her. But it's not like he belongs to her, is it? I just can't believe it. But Cornelia won't stop whispering to Remo. Gorda, the spy, must turn her attention to Peter. She barely understands his German, or is she just not listening to him? What are they whispering about? Peter expects an answer.

"Yeah, yeah," Gorda says. Or was she supposed to say "no, no"?

Remo turns toward the water, thank God.

"What do you do?" Peter asks. Or did he ask: "What do you read"?

"Pardon? I don't always understand what you say," Gorda says.

Peter laughs with untiring friendliness. But Gorda has no eyes or ears for him.

"Remo," she calls out, "doesn't the city look particularly pretty from here?"

He turns around. Cornelia takes him by his arm again, but he frees himself. His counter movement was distinctly obvious—or did he just happen to reach for a branch? With a leaf in hand, laughing lips, and tightened eyebrows, Remo approaches: what made him angry, Gorda thinks. I hope it wasn't me.

"Indeed, the view of the city is particularly pretty from here," Remo says. Only then, does Gorda dare to look at the city, to look at it for real.

Why am I observing Remo? Because he is working on his Ph.D. in German and doesn't look like a scholar of German. That is, he doesn't have the excessive forehead of a thinker and reader, nor does he have a stalk-like slim body. He also lacks the glassy polished look. His shoulders broadly extend in a masculine manner as though they mean to spread inexhaustible strength. His hands are large and charge-taking like those of a supreme commander. And with these hands he intends to turn thousands of pages? And with these shoulders he intends to live bent over words? And with these arms to carry knowledge home? Shouldn't he rather be a Roman general or a Swiss mercenary or a talented long-thrower athlete at the Olympics?

I, at least, see him on the back of a mighty warhorse, lance in his hand or how he unyieldingly forces down a wild lion in an arena. "Victory! Victory!" the crowd shouts.

"He doesn't look like a scholar of German at all," Gorda says when she is alone with Cornelia. But he wants to be like his brother, and this beautiful body is supposed to be dissolved into intellect: his shoulders and hands, his gorgeous full Italian hair, all of this—everything—is supposed to remain unused, to be ruined, to serve a library of thousands of books. That's actually too bad, Gorda thinks. Such a body is much too good to become a professor. How weak Hans, her juvenile crush, appears in comparison. And Gorda thinks about his thin legs and meager arms, and how she loved and caressed him. An image of misery. An image of pain. Away with you, image; here too dwell love and life.

The next day, they take a boat trip together. Cornelia clings to Remo, really, she is clinging to him.

Remo's eyebrows are pulled together and only start relaxing when Cornelia says to Peter: "All right, Peter, the two of us will go and get some wine."

Is he happy to be alone with Gorda or to be getting some wine soon? Remo moves closer to her and explains the vineyards. "Look, Gorda," he says because they are on familiar first-name terms by now, "there are fallow terraces in between, and these terraces are ancient. My God, how the people bend down so much to work in this kind of vineyard. They're really steep. The terraces protect the soil from slipping down and the people as well, it seems to me."

Now Gorda takes a close look of the vineyards, which she could barely notice before because she had to focus on Remo, on his beamlike tomcat-eyebrows, and the corners of his mouth, which kept shifting between merriment and mockery.

Without Remo and without Peter, I would've had a much nicer time with Cornelia, Gorda thinks in a suddenly sad mood. We'd be sitting here drinking wine and friendship and vistas in big gulps, but now I'm angry when Cornelia returns with two glasses of wine and says: "Peter will be right here, too." She hands a glass to Remo and raises her glass to him: "Here's to us," she says, and I know that she does not mean me. What do they have going on between them? Gorda thinks listlessly. This tall, masculine man and my petite, plump girl friend, who reaches up to his chest—that just doesn't fit together. Thank God, there's Peter with the wine, that conceals everything, and Gorda drinks down the pain—a kind of pressure here and there and where her heart could be. And she can laugh again! Now she is already snorting with laughter and giggling. "Well, Peter, listen up," she says, "is it you who speaks German, or is it me who speaks German?—someone is in error here."

Peter laughs cheerfully, and Remo's eyebrows turn into beams again before he explains the origins of Swiss German. It is, he says, an earlier form of High German, rescued from the Middle Ages in a manner of speaking, earlier but in no way inferior."

"And you will study Middle High German one day; then you'll understand Peter better."

Now Gorda blushes. Remo explains and explains. Obviously, he just reaches into a brain library that is filled to the brim while her brain is empty because she spent the summer lying in the meadows instead of being eye, ear, and note-taking hand in the amphitheater.

You'll never amount to anything, says a voice in her. And up there, on the left side, something presses against her forehead. And a scratching and shuffling begins. "The rat, the rat," Gorda exclaims in terror.

"What, a rat?" Cornelia yells in disgust. "Where is it?"

The men rush forward, ready to protect.

"Nonsense," Gorda groans. "I just mean: my head hurts. I've got to go home immediately. Or would you by chance have any pain pills on you, Cornelia? No, strong ones, I need really strong ones. Oh my God, the rat is there."

Gorda is in bed early. Pillow over her eyes; her ears gummed up. "Yes yes, Cornelia, go out with those two." And she thinks: three's better than four; this way, everyone is watching everyone else.

The last day as a foursome. They plan to spend it celebrating and playing. Oh, how beautiful July is! Risen from the rat's bed, as though there were no migraine and no inner voice, Gorda laughs into the warm air. And she really doesn't care when Cornelia attaches herself to Remo's arm, and it's really all the same to her when Peter gives a wrong answer. Today I'm so full of joy! And she takes Peter's arm as though it were Remo's, and she barely notices when Cornelia kisses Remo's cheek. Surely, that had to be a joke.

Cornelia spreads the blanket and places onto it the bottle of wine, the bowls with potato salad and bread and salami. And they eat as though they had known each other forever and would never let go of each other. They spend the last evening in a garden restaurant with lanterns in the tree branches and candles on the bottles. When Cornelia is dancing cheek-to-shoulder with Peter, Remo moves closer to Gorda again, although he had belonged to Cornelia all day. "When are you leaving for home?" He asks quietly but not too quietly. "The day after tomorrow," she quickly says because somebody could come. "Meet me tomorrow evening alone, do you hear me, alone," he says assertively. "I'll pick you up at seven."

Gorda nods and looks at Peter and Cornelia to see whether they have caught the betrayal. But they are happily dancing with their eyes closed and ears filled with music and tongues loosened by wine.

The next day, Cornelia has to go the university. Before she leaves, Gorda tells her: "Remo wants to go out with me tonight, just the two of us. I hope you don't mind."

"No," Cornelia says vehemently and, for no reason, slams the door behind her.

Gorda sleeps in until the afternoon: sleep makes you beautiful. Lots of sleep makes you more beautiful, and Gorda absolutely needs to become more beautiful. Meticulously, she paints a face onto her face. Oh, if only I didn't need to paint. This way, all my beauty can be caressed away or kissed away.

At six o'clock Cornelia is back. "Well, you look ready to dance," and she laughs snidely or sadly. And she adds: "By the way, I've changed my mind. I will be joining you. Because I never told you that I ... well, that he ... well, that we ..."

Gorda interrupts her hastily: "But you said that he's too grumpy for you. And with me he's never been grumpy."

"I'll be joining you, regardless," Cornelia says.

"No, you won't," Gorda says.

"Yes, I will too," Cornelia says and slams the bathroom door behind herself with this meaning: that's my last word. This is not a last word: that's Gorda's vow to herself.

Half an hour later Cornelia emerges from the bathroom ready to dance and to reconcile. "Let's have a glass of wine," she says, "a glass to make peace." Gorda drinks to make war.

"I've got to go," she says and puts on her coat.

"I'll come with you,"

"No, I'll stay home then. You or I —both of us, that won't work."

Right at this moment, there's a knock on the door.

"Well, how was it?" Cornelia asks, and her backs arched as though she had to jump.

"Just imagine," Gorda says, "he told me that he had been studying me intently every minute. Everything I did or neglected to do, he was able to describe to me. Whenever I gazed at the Rhine, his gaze followed mine. And whenever he exchanged words in Swiss-German with Peter, he heard my standard German. And whenever he admired the town, he examined my profile. Isn't that funny?"

"And you, were you also able to tell him everything he did and neglected to do?" Cornelia asks and her half-moon eyes glow like two sharp-edged sickles.

"What do you mean by that?"

"Well, I did notice that you weren't able to take your eyes off him."

And with her sickles Cornelia mows down Gorda's firm voice until Gorda's only able to whisper:

"He said he's fallen in love with me."

"And you probably feel the same way?"

Cornelia straightens her back, she opens her eyes wide, and takes cover behind her mug filled with coffee:

You and I, we will part ways, she certainly is thinking now.

Is Remo worth breaking up with my dear friend? Gorda wonders.

Now say "no" immediately; I don't feel that I've fallen in love with him.

But I do feel that way too. And I don't want to go through the agony of choosing one or the other. I want my girlfriend to the left of me and Remo to the right of me—each human being has two sides.

"Yes, I feel that way too," Gorda finally says. "You always thought he was too grumpy, don't you remember? And with me, he's not grumpy at all. Maybe, the two of you weren't a good match—but he and I, we're a good match. Give us a chance," Gorda pleads with Cornelia.

Really, she is pleading. But actually she's not pleading for Remo; she's pleading for Cornelia.

At this moment, her friend lets go of the mug she had been clutching, and it loudly crashes on the floor. Suddenly, Gorda hears sobbing.

"Oh, Cornelia, nothing's happened?" she says.

"Oh yes, it has," Cornelia sobs.

But Gorda knows that she won. She's won Cornelia back. And in the afternoon, she takes the train home.

———

Remo's first letter: it's a package, a forty-page long package. His handwriting, small and jagged and as if drawn with ink, page after page writing like a Chinese picture. Gorda lies down in her bed to read: this is the beginning of a novel, so take your time. She's afraid of this novel. What could the unfamiliar man be telling her for forty pages? How long do her answers have to be? If he is able to write forty pages to an unfamiliar woman, how long will his letters be when he knows her better? And later his complaints: why don't you also describe your thoughts, your feelings, your movement in all their trivial and pivotal details— and doesn't that mean that, from now on, I will be sitting at my desk and composing letters when I should be listening to knowledge in the amphitheater? And do I really like to describe my innermost feelings? Yes, I do when I talk with Cornelia or with Marion, but not with a fountain pen because that's so slow, and the first draft is never well written, this means forty pages twice a week or even only twice a month—I can't manage that: I am certainly not the right woman for this so well-written man. Tomorrow, I will sit down and write: This isn't working. Forty pages are too long, even for a declaration of love that I think should be kept short: I love you or I just can't forget you, but no such tapeworm oaths and dinosaur thoughts on the topic of love.

And now forty pages come fluttering into her home every day. Gorda reads and hears page after page, which become increasingly longer. There is no end of a page in sight. You'll need days for a package, no, years! And she has to go to class and can't lie here and read, read a life away.

At that moment, she wakes up with a sigh.

And the letter, I'd rather read it tomorrow.

A trip to Salzburg with little Anni. Her dear cousin no longer laughs like a whistling buoy, she remains silent as though behind walls. Her pretty blonde head only briefly looks through the barred window: I'm not telling you anything, the down-turned corners of her mouth indicate. And Gorda says to herself: Well, that's fine, I'm not going to tell you anything either.

Anni has to stop in Munich because she has to tell her boyfriend's sister something.

"Please, don't ask me what it's about," Anni says.

"That's your loss," Gorda deflects the blows—but making sure it's done on the inside; you show nothing on the outside.

Salzburg, Austria

This promises to be a wonderful vacation! Had I only stayed home. So you talk about the weather, the food, the countryside. Anni barely reads any books—or not any of the books Gorda reads. Gorda hides her chagrin in her book: in this book the author looks into people's heads as though with an X-ray beam that doesn't illuminate gyri of the brain but rather those of the soul. If Anni were in front of him, what would he have described? He would have removed stone after stone of the wall that surrounds her. And suddenly, he would have stood before her in person, and she would have flung her arms around his neck: My savior, she would have called out. And then she would have taken her thoughts and feelings and hoisted them on top of the tower like a flag and, quite carelessly, let it flop back and forth in the wind.

But she doesn't do that with me. And the page to Remo remains empty. You just can't write all the time: "My cousin doesn't say a word to me." So you describe the visit to Mozart's house and the stroll through the Mirabell Gardens and the pretty shops with traditional Austrian clothing and the excursion to Lake Mondsee and the excursion to Lake Ossiach.

And my little Anni always keeps her silence. Then Gorda writes: "I think this trip was a mistake."

Two days later Remo calls her in the guest house: "Come and visit me in Bunten," he says. "My mother is out of town."

"That would work," Gorda says. "My cousin doesn't need me."

When Gorda tells Anni: "I'm going to go visit Remo in Bunten," Anni flings open the castle gate for the first time: "What? You want to leave me here all alone. You've got to be crazy!"

But Gorda isn't crazy—she must visit Remo, where she can talk and laugh and be young. Silence makes you grow old. The following day she goes there. And she knows that this will not be the last time she goes there.

Now she can tell Remo about her book and her loneliness in Salzburg, and about what kind of prodigy Mozart was as a child and how you explain prodigies. And why my cousin doesn't speak with me. And what did she tell Klaus' sister? And why some people make such a big deal of secrecy. What is so special about the experiences of one person? Other people have experiences, too; and they are offended and humiliated and overconfident and sick. But walls—they are deadly. And silence—it makes you grow old.

———

Remo's apartment is roomy and dark like winter. Outside, the summer afternoon dances in a warm light, and November is coming. But you don't want to turn on the lamps because it's just three in the afternoon.

"My father bought this piece of furniture. It came from a palace," Remo says. "And this piece of furniture comes from a farmhouse and this carpet from an auction and this picture from the artist himself."

The huge apartment is decked out in chests and wall closets, in earthenware and brass candle holders, in seas of Persian carpets and Persian rug runners: This is a museum—created by father and grandfather and mother for eternal remembrance, this way and no other.

"You've got to leave everything the way it is," whispers the old clock above the fireplace, which is rarely used.

"Your living room looks pretty crammed," Gorda says. But Remo's eyebrows move toward each other, and his mouth laughs without laughing. So Gorda doesn't say anything anymore. It's better to listen the wrong way than to say the right thing. There is a big difference between my finding the apartment crammed or his finding it crammed. And it isn't just crammed; it's also crammed in an impressive way. In the hallway there's a long stretch of wall filled with books.

"Oh, so many beautiful books. I could spend years reading here."

Finally, the upper and lower halves of Remo's face laugh at the same time, and Gorda feels welcome.

When Remo shows her his room, she knows: I want to live this way forever! This is the most beautiful room I know. It's

One wall in Remo's room

not a bedroom; it's a library. Three walls are completely covered with books. And along the forth wall, as if by accident, there is an old carved wooden bed. In the middle, there is a large desk full of books and loose pages. In his typewriter, there is a page that begins with words: "A study of the poet Conrad Ferdinand Meyer as a critic may be surprising ..."

"Leave that alone," Remo says. "That's the beginning of my dissertation, and I've been rewriting it for days. But while you're here, I'm not interested in it at all. Come on, I'll make you a cup of coffee and cut off a slice of the braided brioche for each of us."

After the coffee, Gorda unpacks her things in the room where she will sleep. This, too, is a room according to her taste: the two beds next to the walls are covered with light blue comforters, and light blue curtains adorn the window. In the middle of the room, there is an old, narrow rustic table with a rustic lamp on it. Warmth and well-being prevail in here while winter storms roar out there. But actually, out there, August and sunny joy prevail.

"Remo, please show me the town. I've been looking so much forward to Bunten."

"Tomorrow," Remo says. "We'll do all of that tomorrow." And then he takes her into his arms.

Oh yes, warmth and well-being—who needs the town.

The sightseeing tour through town takes place the next day. Remo is the guide, and Gorda allows herself to be guided. She feels in the hands of a safe guide. He knows which streetcar to take and which way to go. They get off at the train station, where a colonnade begins, and inside there's one shop after the other. But Gorda isn't able to pay any attention to them because she has to tell Remo about everything she saw in Salzburg. This way, she sees Salzburg as she is looking at Bunten.

"Come, let's just go for a drink," Remo says, and they sit down in a café with a view of the river and the long Urban Bridge and, beyond it, peaks of the Alps like threatening fingers in the sky. Those peaks could also be hands waving in the distance. Gorda calmly drinks her glass of wine. Remo's eyebrows rest peacefully next to each other like two sleeping lambs, and his lips glisten full and rosy in the sunlight. And Gorda feels: I am protected here. Nothing can happen to me here. Remo's strong hands rest on the table, always ready to hold her, to lead her, and show her the way and not let her go.

What weak hands did Hans have in contrast! Never again weak legs and weak arms and weak love.

The most beautiful thing is that Remo looks like a man and talks like a professor of German literature. Right now he is lecturing about Conrad Ferdinand Meyer, who's been his interest for years. And he relates an anecdote about this famous man, such a quirky incident, and it seems as though we were laughing about a dear friend who lives just two blocks from us. And then he tells me about good old Cornelia. He just calls her "good old Cornelia" as though she weren't quite good enough or only good and nothing else, and this calms Gorda because these two didn't after all …

"Oh well, that was nothing," Remo says with determination. "That was just a winter whim. And didn't Cornelia have this old head teacher?"

So Gorda laughs about good old Cornelia like about a once dear friend. But "once" isn't over yet.

They walk through narrow, little streets that get even more narrow. "This is old town," Remo says. "It dates back to the Middle Ages."

These dark streets wind up and down until they become ever more narrow and gloomy.

"You've got the darkest Middle Ages here," she explains laughing.

"Of course, we didn't have war here, and without war, you too would still have Middle Ages and Renaissance and Baroque in abundance. But you always had to go to war."

Remo's eyebrows are staring like a wooden beam. So Gorda quickly addresses a new topic: "Please tell me about

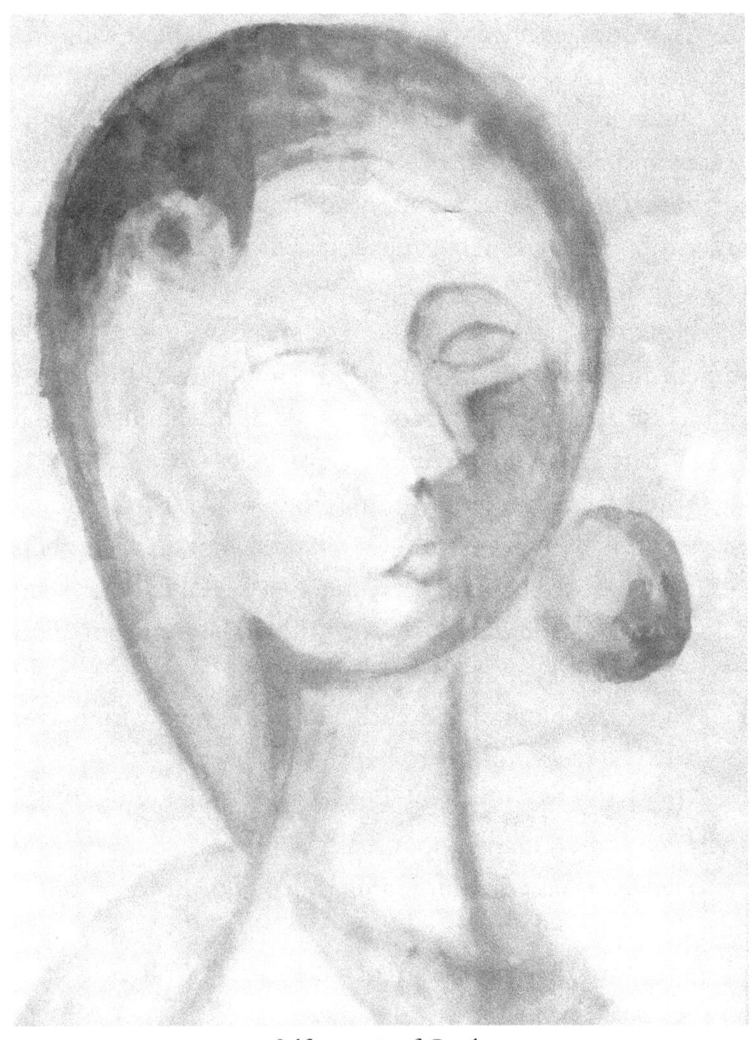

Self portrait of Gorda

your mother," she says. And Remo forgets about Middle Ages, Renaissance, and the war.

"Oh yes, my mother, she's quite a character. You've got to get to know her yourself. She's willpower that's become flesh."

And Gorda is filled with horror at the thought of willpower become flesh. Or is it just the narrow streets that frighten her?

Suddenly, they are no longer standing in front of squat houses and gloomy, narrow streets but in front of a powerfully soaring cathedral. You lift your head all the way up and back in order to look up as high as possible, but the cathedral is even higher than high.

"This too is the Middle Ages," Remo says, willpower become stone. And they walk into the stony Middle Ages. Inside, it is scoured spick and span and contains very little altar decoration.

"Where are all the pictures?" Gorda asks.

"They were removed during the Reformation," Remo answers full of knowledge. "Our church doesn't care about curlicues and scrollwork. Everything here needs to be cool and bare so that people in church don't think about art but about their creator and about Zwingli, his prophet."

"But a few pictures and curlicues would help with prayer; this way you have nothing to look at."

"The point is not to look but to pray," Remo says. "Work and pray, and do that without many words."

Silence makes you old, Gorda thinks. I want to get out of this place quickly.

"From up there, our citizens take their own lives." Remo points up to a protrusion of the tower.

"Does this happen a lot?" Gorda asks appalled.

"At least twice a year. We had just one this year, so the second one is walking around here somewhere."

And Gorda looks, her eyes showing her concern, at the people who hurry through the narrow streets—no, actually, they don't hurry; they walk deliberately and carefully as though they had to move enormous obstacles out of their way, rocks and old tree stumps. And yet the street lies as though swept clean.

"They also come from the Middle Ages," Gorda says, "and enter modern times so slowly that they have just made it to the nineteenth century."

"What strange remarks you sometimes make," Remo says, and Gorda knows that he is proud of her remarks. As though he himself had thought them. And she resolves to always make strange remarks so that Remo is proud of her and doesn't confuse her with good old Cornelia or good old Elke or good old Erika or whatever the names of his girlfriends might have been. The butt of a rifle hits Gorda right in her chest: this young girl there could have been his girlfriend or that one with the brown pigtails or the blonde with the bob. What is it that Remo is looking at? At the mouths of girls or the rows of houses, at the colorfully painted sculptures of fountains or at the backs of knees that peek out from under short skirts? It is best to talk as fast as a weasel, so he has to look at her and listen to her. She wants to tear all these images from his breast so that bleakness and cleanliness may rule there, and then she will place only one image into it—her own.

"What strange remarks you always make," Remo says, and his eyebrows are at rest like two peaceful lambs.

At home at Remo's place—it is a little bit her home too—she takes a book from his gorgeous wall of books. On the first page, it says in English: *Dear Remo, this book will teach you to understand women, Lisa.*

Who is Lisa?

The book burns blazing hot in my hands. This apartment is not my apartment, and Remo is not my Remo: his breast is filled with old images.

"Who's Lisa," Gorda asks quickly as Remo returns from the cellar with a bottle of wine.

"Oh, good old Lisa," Remo says, and her burden of pain is lifted in the air like a cheerful balloon, and she barely listens as he explains: "She wanted to marry me, an American girl, and she eventually flew home. But before she left, she told me: *You don't understand women, you know.*"

The main thing is that he doesn't belong to Lisa, Gorda thinks. She will teach him to understand women herself, but by no means all women, just her. For this purpose, she has come to Bunten; for this purpose, she takes him into her arms; for this purpose, she will read his books and even, if necessary, endure willpower become flesh. But until then there's still time: first of all, she'll leave for home tomorrow. And then there were three little drops of blood in the bed—not more, that was all, and Remo said, "I love you." And for that, the fight with Hans had been worth it: now she finally has a past. And it's the right kind of past—at the same time, it is always the future.

Remo gave her his gold signet ring, which she now wears on a necklace. In California this means: *she is going steady.* In Europe, there is no real name for a ring around one's neck, but it makes so much sense. Let the people on the train look at it as peculiarly as they want to. When she holds the ring in her hand, then she holds Remo in her hand. Sometimes the ring lies on her chest and against her neck and in her hair. And the ring is almost as beautiful as a kiss or a glance or an I-love-you and, for a long while now, it has to stand in for reality and be dream and promise. The promise that Remo isn't somewhere at this moment saying: "Oh well, good old Gorda."

And she practices Remo on a piece of paper, Remo Luck, and again and again Remo Luck and sometimes Gorda Luck, when no one is looking. And it's easy to write and feels like it belongs together: Gorda and Remo's Luck.

"You've got quite a winning name, Remo," she said, back then in Bonn at Cornelia's. "It's got to be good luck to have the name Luck."

"Or maybe bad luck," Cornelia objected. "Man should not tempt the gods."

"A name won't tempt the gods," Remo retorted. "A name is not a human being, after all."

And still: Gorda Luck—wouldn't that be like Gorda-in-luck?

Sometime a name knows more than we humans.

———

There is no luck without punishment. During her vacation, Gorda has to work and pay for her days in Salzburg. Yet she isn't just paying for Salzburg but also for Bunten, and she gladly pays for such luck.

Dad managed to place her with the Cattle Breed Registry because of his business connections with the director. The latter wants to honor Dad by giving work to the daughter, but he has no work for her, so a remedy has to be found.

"Isn't there anything to do here?" He asked the secretary in charge.

And lo and behold, something is found after two days of carrying letters back and forth, making coffee, and dusting. Gorda will now cross out the numbers of the cows that died or were eaten or sold, and add those that were newly acquired or born. Each rancher has his own card file. Yes, how easy this work is during the first hour: comparing numbers, deleting numbers, writing numbers. Miss Carstens, what time is it? Two more hours until lunch break. Comparing numbers, placing numbers. Thank God, it's finally lunch time. You go and get a coffee and a bologna sandwich. This takes at least forty minutes. Oh, the fresh air of Oldenburg! If only I could visit Cornelia. But it's better not to return too late to the long concrete building with the cow card files. Comparing numbers, deleting numbers, writing numbers. What time is it, Miss Carstens? You do have your own watch! But it doesn't seem to be working quite right today. The hands of the watch don't move like they usually do. By now I've compared, deleted, and added hundreds of cows and the long day is still an early afternoon. My eyes are overflowing with numbers. And now a paralysis of my right hand, the cow-hand, begins to set in, no, it's just my index finger and thumb that won't work. How this ball-point pen chafes!

Comparing numbers, deleting numbers, writing numbers.

In the evening, you don't have the strength left for Beethoven or Aida. Gorda now listens to pop songs, songs she had never heard before. She's catching up on her days as a teenager. Didn't Doris always love "Love me tender" while she herself listened to "Celeste Aida" or the alto rhapsody by Brahms: Ah, who heals the pains of him whose balm turned to poison …

For her, too, the balm of work turns increasingly to poison with each day. For ten days in Salzburg and four days in Bunten, she has to do eight weeks of compulsory labor; that's how poorly the recording of cows pays. If it weren't for the gold ring, she'd hardly be able to remember Bunten, Remo's lamb-and-beam eyebrows, his tenderness and his pride when he says: "What strange remarks you sometimes make." At the moment, she can't think of any such remarks. Whoever compares and deletes and adds numbers on a daily basis can't think and say anything strange. That person only utters what is most necessary, like butter and bread are for a starving person. Artichokes and caviar will not satisfy the hunger of such a person. Every day, she has these bread-and-butter conversations with Miss Carstens.

"What time is it? Does my watch really show the correct time?"

"Where are we going to buy lunch today?"

"When is the director going home?"

"Isn't it five o'clock already?"

And in the evening, she only says: "I've got to go to bed right away."

And despite her exhaustion, she can't fall asleep. Four thousand three hundred ninety-eight, her brain counts. Four thousand three hundred ninety-nine, her brain counts. Four thousand four hundred. Four thousand four hundred and one. Stop, stop, Gorda yells in her sleep. But she can't hear that anymore.

***

Gorda arrives after Marion, who sits on a bed on one side of the room and gnaws on a fountain pen. Next to her is pile of letters.

"What are you doing?" Gorda asks surprised because sweaters, skirts, underwear, and shoes are piled up around Marion.

"Oh, I'm just dashing a line to Peter," she says.

Across from Marion is Gorda's piece of the room: a bed, a wardrobe, a chair, and table. What else do you need to be lonely?

Feeling lonely, Gorda takes her clothes out of the suitcase, the university clothes, books, and woolen sweaters. It's winter in Tübingen.

Marion finally closes her envelope and, with a lonely stare, looks into the air. Gorda lights a friendship candle and suggests a cup of tea. While drinking tea and eating cookies and talking about Salzburg and Bunten, and about Peter and Remo, they postpone their loneliness for about an hour or so.

They aren't lonely as such; they are lonely together. If we could at least put up a curtain across the room, but this way I always see Marion's glass-blue eyes, which search the walls for sentences to include in her letters to Peter. Marion doesn't just write things down, she drafts and redrafts and drafts anew. Page by page, the pile next to her bed grows: that's the draft pile. At the back of her bed lies a dictionary from which she gathers words for her knowledgeable treatises to Peter. Or, perhaps, she describes me and how I'm lying here, trying to concentrate on Möricke's life, although I'm peering at her and her letter pile and at her skirts and underwear, which she still hasn't put away.

People should also remain with one foot firmly grounded in what is real and reliable. Science is more reliable than pretty sentences. Therefore, Gorda doesn't want to study just literature but also a science about human beings—psychology. And doesn't one subject complement the other in a most perfect way? Armed with my scientific knowledge of human beings, I approach the texts of world literature and assess the presentation of characters with the help of valuable data and the art of statistics.

For the art of statistics, I first have to buy a math book. And I had thought that I had left the annoying arithmetic behind me after high school. Now it starts anew: yet this time it is supposed to allow me to tap into the human soul. This is no longer a simple chart that I am holding here but rather a magic key in the hand of a pioneer and expert. And Gorda wants to be such a pioneer and expert of both soul and sentences. For this purpose, she has to navigate valleys and mountains of numbers and equations. The goal is worth the painstaking climb, and I emerge from the lowlands and lack of understanding and ascend to refreshing enlightenment at as of yet unimagined heights.

She wants to know why, on certain days, she lies about like Marion, the letter writer, as though ill and is unable to find her way to the amphitheater, although she had firmly resolved: tomorrow I will get up at seven. But then it's nine o'clock again, and Marion is drinking tea and writing the first draft of her first letter of the new week. And instead of beginning the morning in fresh snow, you walk through streets that are already fully muddied up.

On other days, however, she can't be in the cold shower early enough, although the landlord had promised warm water, and she hurries to the empty amphitheater and boldly decides on a seat in the front row instead of modestly slinking toward the back rows. And she promises herself: Just like this and no other way every day. And that's what she does. For three days. On the fourth day, Marion says: "Oh, why don't you just sleep in." And she actually does sleep in although she just thought: Sleeping in—no, never! And she waits for mail like Marion, for mail from Mom and for mail from Cornelia, but above all, for mail from Remo. And Marion waits for mail from Peter. On days, when both of them receive mail, they sit across from each other and rustle with the pages. Marion sucks at her fountain pen and immediately begins with different variations of responses, while Gorda has her hand clasped around the gold signet ring and doesn't feel like writing.

She always feels like getting letters and reading letters but never like writing them. But whoever wants to receive sentences must also write sentences. Why is it that she—who loves to read and talk and listen and think—doesn't enjoy writing?

Because each letter is an evaluation—an evaluation or a devaluation. This is how I write, and doesn't Remo write much better or good old Cornelia or Lisa or Marion, perhaps. I'd rather not even think about Mörike and Keller and C. F. Meyer.

So just read this precious sample of a sentence: His head was covered with a light brown wig that was cut off in a straight line across his forehead …

These are words too, quite normal words, put together gracefully and and adding up to literature. World literature, even. And now don't be afraid anymore: boldly place one sentence after the other, continue quickly in this manner because you still want to go to the library to look for an important work on the secret of writing. After all, this book—that will loosen the cramp in your hand and turns your tongue into your quill—must exist somewhere. If the way of my thoughts went directly to the page, I would fill thousands of manuscript pages, and among the thousands of sentences, there certainly would be a few hundred groundbreaking sentences. These I would filter out and press onto a special page, and after many years, they would add up to the comfort of my life: Look, you wrote this yourself and it could not be more beautiful. But why do I need such comfort? And why am I studying the science of the human soul? Because I want to know why I can't live without the comfort of beautiful sentences.

There is now a new medication, Remo wrote, absolutely safe. My friend, who is in med school, will get it for me. And I will send it to you.

She expects a small package, a compact parcel, but instead a huge box arrives, and as she opens it, Marion watches her. As long as Marion doesn't notice what's in here, Gorda thinks. Nervously, she takes book after book out of the strange package, which is to provide for both mental nourishment and her bodily sterility at the same time. Oh, there at the back, the secret is rattling, and she quickly grasps it to prevent it from rattling as Marion contently hurries with one of the books to her part of the room.

"This is a great book," Marion says. "I've definitely got to read it."

"Go ahead and read it," Gorda says, glad to know her secret is safe in her purse. When Marion goes downtown, I'll take a look at it.

Twenty-one pills. I'll never be like Margarete from Goethe's play. My concerns turn to where they belong: to my university studies, and my dreams turn to Remo—without the fear that he is Faust and has the devil by his side or in his body. Twenty-one pills per month, and I will and won't be myself: "I and you and it." It'll be a long while until "the three of us."

Oh, joy, Remo wants to meet her in Grindelwald before Christmas. He rented a mountain cottage there from a fraternity brother. Gorda packs winter boots and winter sweater: Grindelwald is covered in deep snow, Remo wrote.

Grindelwald in winter

What a nuisance, the cottage is frozen shut; Remo first has to hack the door open before they are able to enter with wet feet, bags, and hands. There's snow inside just as there is outside. Remo begins to sweep and scour. Disappointed, Gorda sits down on the chair by the window and looks outside: instead of sky, saw-tooth mountains and, left and right, dark brown cottages and everywhere gorgeous untouched snow. No reason to be disappointed. Once Remo gets the heater going, Gorda forgets her feet and hands and the snow on the stove top. Remo says, "don't touch a thing; I'll get this done by myself. And she is allowed to watch him putting sheets on the beds—sheets that his mother had given him, and a package with bread and butter and assorted Bündner cold cuts.

"Of course, she doesn't know that I'm not here by myself," Remo giggles. Indeed, he giggles in a way that doesn't match his strong shoulders. "Then she wouldn't have been as attentive."

"Of course not," Gorda says. And thinks: Why of course not?

<hr>

Christmas at home in Oldenburg. Now she no longer stands alone in front of the tree, and she doesn't go to church alone, and she doesn't eat Christmas marzipan alone: whenever she touches Remo's ring, she's never alone. And she is able to hold it in her hand all day long and twist it around her finger and let it swing on its necklace. Cornelia says: "What kind of bulky ring is that you're wearing?" And she tells her: "That's Remo's ring." And Cornelia just looks away, turns, and wants to go home, although she is supposed to stay until six. And she doesn't mention the ring anymore. But went they are in the opera, she shows Gorda an envelope, she holds it up just for a second and then puts it away again: "Look, I got a letter from Remo."

And as though the knife had missed its mark, she adds: "I have twenty more of them."

Up above on the left side, pressure starts to spread, and the prelude begins. As the curtain rises, a couple of feet begin to scuffle. No, they don't scuffle; they run roughshod around in her head.

"The rat," Gorda whispers, "my God, the rat."

And she rustles with the papers in her purse. Where did I put the pills? "Shh," a voice behind her hisses. I've got to get out of here, Gorda knows. There are fewer people on the left than on the right. So she goes left.

With her back bent and her hand on the rat, she stumbles and steps past people's legs.

The next morning, she writes Remo with only one question: Why did Cornelia get a letter from you?

But it takes a long time until a response can reach her. At least four days, and those four days must be lived and slept and worked through. She puts the ring into a drawer; it just burns her fingers. Now she stares at the tree alone, and she goes into the kitchen alone, and she eats Christmas chocolate alone. Forever alone. Ah, I can't stand it. Pressure begins to build on the top left side.

"Immediately take a pill for migraine," her doctor in Oldenburg had advised. She takes a pill immediately.

Monday at nine in the morning, Monday at three in the afternoon, Monday at seven in the evening, Tuesday at eleven in the morning, Tuesday at five in the afternoon, Tuesday around ten in the evening.

Mom says: "You're crazy. You'll get sick if you go on like this." But she's already sick.

On Wednesday, the phone rings.

"Oh, yes, I'll get her right away," Mom says visibly relieved. Gorda lets the pill drop back into the vial.

"How are you doing. Well, how am I doing? Well, of course." And she knows that she won't need any more pills.

"And the letter"? She asks as Remo keeps talking about snow and very low temperatures.

"The letter doesn't mean a thing. She just asked me for the address of a doctor. She thinks she's pregnant."

"But I don't know anything about it," Gorda stammers. "My best friend, and I don't know anything about it."

<hr>

"Remo called me today," Gorda starts at tea time, barely after closing the door to Cornelia's room behind her.

"He probably told you about the letter," Cornelia says.

"Yes, he did."

"That was stupid stuff," Cornelia says. "I'm not with child, of course not."

Why of course not, Gorda thinks. Did they perhaps after all … But actually, she's just glad that Remo doesn't have to write letters to Cornelia anymore. And she still has twenty more of those. Twenty pieces of memory without me.

There's a letter from Remo already waiting in Tübingen.

"Come and visit me in two weeks. My mother will be traveling then."

She's still unpacking and already packing up again. Through new snow and old, she walks to the amphitheater, but in her thoughts, she's packing her travel bag or suitcase. Is it enough to take an extra sweater, or do I need two and the green dress, or is this not necessary at all because we won't be going anywhere? The professor reads from his prepared pages, and Gorda's writing hand writes along, but her head isn't writing along; it plans and rejects; it washes and goes shopping.

"What an effort you expend for a couple of days," Marion says as she sucks sentences for Peter from her fountain pen. "I'd just take the travel bag. That's all you need."

So Gorda takes the bag. It's ridiculous to take a suitcase for just a couple of days. Remo might think I came to stay.

The train ride is long but not as long as the one from Oldenburg. From there, Gorda would take a night train. But this way, she boards around lunch time and arrives in the evening. With her small travel bag in hand: Look, I didn't come to stay.

Remo is standing on the platform and, with delight, takes the nothing of a bag from her. "You know how to restrain yourself," he says, and Gorda is glad about the compliment. It's good that he has no inkling that she wanted to take along the green dress and two more sweaters that she had gotten for Christmas. It's just for Remo that she now gets sweaters as presents for Christmas. It's just for Remo that she saves money for clothes from the money she has left after rent and food. That's why she lives in the corner of a room and not in a room.

"I've got to tell you something unpleasant," Remo giggles in the streetcar, which he calls tram, or perhaps it is something unpleasant. "No doubt," he giggles. And his giggling doesn't go with his drawn together eyebrows. His eyebrows say that it is very unpleasant for me that I have to tell you this.

"So just spit it out." Gorda intensely inhales the air made humid by the snow. Certainly, I'll have to leave again tomorrow!

"My mother is at home, you know. She isn't traveling at all."

"But you told me …"

"Yes, she had wanted to. But then she felt the weather was too bad."

"And why didn't you warn me?"

"But I was so looking forward to your visit. And you've got to meet her sometime anyway …"

Oh, my god, the slippers! Gorda has only brought slippers: the boots she's wearing and slippers. Because she had thought we're going to be inside the house all day long. And alone. And now the willpower become flesh is there, and I've got to face it in slippers. If only I hadn't listened to Marion and instead had packed the suitcase as planned—it would have had the black flats in it and the green dress and a sweater for each day. She must think I've come to stay.

When Gorda unpacks her bits and pieces, they are still by themselves.

"But she'll be here soon," Remo says. "You don't need to be afraid." Of course, she needs to be afraid. Who isn't afraid of meeting the woman whom you don't want to meet under any circumstances because of her son who belongs to her and who belongs to you. Perhaps, you'll find out that he doesn't belong to you at all. We Ourselves, that's what Remo's mother calls their family: We Ourselves must stick together.

Whatever sticks together keeps you out.

And now she stands in slippers in front of the woman while she would like to stand in front of her in the green dress and flats, dressed in a way, after all, for a visit with a woman whom you don't know but whom you will get to know, whether you want to or not. And you'd rather show up prepared with your gleaming Sunday best.

Instead, I'm standing her in front of her like a gaping wound.

I hope she doesn't notice the fur trim on my slippers. She's got to think I've come to stay.

Remo's mother is short and hefty, with reddish fuzz on her head. She holds out her hand to Gorda graciously or ungraciously—who can tell the difference—a hand with bent fingertips. My God, she's old, Gorda thinks, much older than my mother. And she remembers his brother, who is fourteen years older, his surrogate father, as Remo called him. Their mother had barely given birth to Remo when her husband died. And all she has left now is this son, and he belongs to her in three ways: he is her husband and her son and also the other son, the professor who is in far-away Bonn.

There's no role for me to play here, Gorda thinks. Except as a visitor. And my slippers contradict that role. I might as well be standing here in my nightgown.

Mother Luck looks down on Gorda as though adorned in a brocade state costume, although she is much shorter than Gorda. And Gorda wonders how she manages to do that. With a slowly moving gaze she examines Gorda: You can't hide anything here, least of all your shame—your slippers.

"Grüezi," she utters the greeting in Swiss German.

Gorda's thoughts mass together like the walls of a fortress. Slippers or not, I do have my pride. And Remo invited me with false words because it was easier for him to lie.

"Do come into the living room," Remo says. "We'll eat dinner."

Bündner cold cuts is what's for dinner. The same variety of cold cuts that Remo's mother had sent with him to Grindelwald. Something she, of course, would not have done if she had known about Gorda. And now she realizes for whom she had packed the cold cuts. And regrets it. For that reason, she eats and remains silent. Or she throws bright blue motherly glances at Remo and talks in riddles, but in riddles only for Gorda. Remo understands immediately, and he nods and laughs, no, he giggles just like he giggles when Gorda says something particularly to the point. He betrays her with every giggle. I have to eat sausage and delicious farmers' bread without being able to taste sausage and farmers' bread. I taste danger. The danger of finding out that Remo doesn't belong to me.

———

However, when she's alone with Remo in her room, he takes her in his arms and comforts her: "Oh, don't take this too seriously. All she's got left is me, and now she feels threatened. You've got to understand. You should have seen how she treated my brother's wife. It was just disgusting."

Yes, just disgusting, Gorda thinks. She's built a disgusting wall of silence for me, and in that wall's shade I'm supposed to shrivel up and die.

"I'd rather leave tomorrow."

Portrait of Remo by Gorda

But she doesn't leave. Remo convinces her to stay: "Don't give a thought to it." But, of course, she has her thoughts when the table is to be cleared, and the mother gets up and says, "Remo," and then Gorda carries bowls and plates to the kitchen. But she says nothing to Gorda. "Chömet, chömet"—come, come—she calls them to lunch when it's time to eat. From that moment on, Swiss German, which is a foreign language for Gorda, pours forth from his mother's mouth although she's certainly able to speak a version of standard German if she wanted to, but she just doesn't want to. Only in her room or his is she together with Remo; outside of both rooms, he doesn't exist anymore: he turns into his mother's son.

———

Remo's mother hadn't always been Remo's mother… hefty with reddish fuzz on her head and bent fingertips. She once was the prettiest farm girl in Deutersheim. At eighteen, she was already married to a handsome farm boy while, at age twenty-two, her older sister still wasn't able to enter the holy state of matrimony. Pretty Elsie had barely given birth to a daughter when a shining non-commissioned officer from the Swiss army rode through Deutersheim. Elsie couldn't get her fill of just looking at him. So she kept looking out of her window hungrier every day. And whoever is hungry also wants something to eat. The bored non-commissioned officer, too, looked more and more daringly at the pretty, young farmwoman because he had nothing else to look at. And boredom is the beginning of many glances.

Elsie wasn't just pretty, but at twenty years of age, she was already willpower become flesh. "That one or no one," she shouted. And threw her herself onto the floor in front of her bewildered parents until they were so ashamed that they decided: not another day in our village. And then Elsie moved away without daughter and without husband, but arm and arm with the daring non-commissioned officer. That is how Remo got his father. And Elsie got a mother-in-law in Bunten who hated her like no one else in this world.

"What does this perfect stranger of a farmgirl want at my sophisticated urban table," she said. "How could my only son get so carried away that he married a divorced woman?"

And only after Remo's brother was born, did she say a word to Elsie. And that was: "We Ourselves must stick together" or something like that. And with that, she meant just the child, herself, and her son, but not Elsie. She was supposed to remain outside. And now Elsie treats her potential daughter-in-law the way she had been treated herself. Only the birth of a grandchild could cause her to dismantle the wall of silence and to say a word to the seductress who has come to take away one of her beloved sons.

"You would think she'd want to spare her daughters-in-law such a date," Gorda told Remo.

"But no," he said, "it's quite normal that people take revenge for having been treated badly."

This means that Remo's mother is normal for not saying one word to Gorda. For whoever stands before her in slippers wants to take away a son; otherwise, he would have told her:

74

Go, put on something decent. Or even better: he would've put her on the train.

In Remo's room, there is a photograph of his mother on the wall. It shows her with full lips, a tiny nose, and her round blue eyes, just like today, even though the tiny nose has turned into a nose and the rounds lips have narrowed with age. Yes, Remo's mother was once a beautiful woman. And she considers herself a beautiful woman still today; there's no doubt about that. And next to this beautiful woman—who got a divorce to marry a daring non-commissioned officer when a divorce was a scandal and nothing else—there stands Gorda, with her small mouth and pointed nose, and certainly no man would risk such a scandal for her. And she wants to take her last son away from her.

"We Ourselves must stick together," Mother Luck says with lips that have become narrow with age. There is no other choice but to leave. And never come back.

"But you'll come back in three months," Remo says, "when you have more time." And wearing flats, Gorda thinks, and in the suitcase the green dress and the new Christmas sweaters. And in her thoughts she's packing again, although she hasn't even left yet.

On the train back to Tübingen, she thinks of Remo's father: his portrait, an oil painting based on a photograph, hangs in his mother's bedroom. In this picture he looks like Remo in profile, but his chin is a little drawn in and his nose is curved more, and he presses his lips together as if he wants to tell his mother for all eternity: And I will marry her. In the Luck family, the sons have to fight for their wives. You respect only what you have fought for. Full of concern, Gorda thinks of Remo's full lips.

In Tübingen, Marion is sucking sentences from her fountain pen for her letters to Peter. But as Gorda enters, she sets her pen aside and asks with interest: "So, how was it?" And Gorda can't hold back and tells her about the divorce, the wall of silence, and Remo's giggling. Marion says; "And that's who you want to marry? I'd rather enter a convent."

"Oh, it is normal for a mother not to want to let go of her son. I just have to be patient."

"Being patient forever," Marion says. "I think highly of my Peter in this respect. He was sent to boarding school when he was only fourteen after his parents separated. And a boarding-school kid like that is at least no mama's boy."

And Remo is never just Remo: he is in a gloomy apartment in Bunten, willpower become flesh called his mother; he is a thousand books on the walls, a rustic bed with blue-flowered sheets, a wall of silence with eyes clear as water that speak in riddles if they speak at all, and he is the man who takes her into his arms and has to protect her from all evils in the world.

From all evils in the world and in Bunten.

———

Apparently, the secrets of the human soul can be computed. It isn't an overgrown forest through which one cuts, with effort, various narrow trails and a few precious clearings, as you had thought, but rather a huge and complicated machinery with a thousand and more screws and turns and levers and rhythms. And whatever it is that rolls and rattles and skips and drones in such a hardly understandable manner—you can still get a handle on it in a surprisingly easy way by means of statistics. Consequently, you present your soul a test full of trick questions, more questions, and follow-up questions concerning its character, then you calculate the sum of the results with the help of statistics, check with the available charts and lists, and divide everything by the necessary remainders—and out comes a personality that is only possible in this manner, likely never to occur again. The whole process takes about an afternoon. If you offer your soul an IQ test the next morning and task it with an aptitude test the following afternoon, you arrive within a few days at a firm image of a potential co-worker, and you don't have to waste years of testing her in the everyday work environment and of putting her under surveillance. How practical for our modern times, where time is also money, and both surprisingly rare. No wonder that industry is extraordinarily interested in the development of test programs that are guaranteed to be error-free. And everywhere in the world—above all in America, though—full-time industrial psychologists are working feverishly on these programs. Can there be any more beautiful work than sitting in front of such a test soul every day and tracking down the secrets of human nature at a quick pace where people used to dawdle? That's when it's worthwhile to pore over a math book and to calculate equations, almost like Hermione, pale and with one's mouth puckered, and having eyes for numbers instead of sentences that are drunken with beauty but consuming time and money.

What the poet achieves in three hundred pages of painstakingly described details, the test psychologist accomplishes in four pages of skilled objective prose, which does not give rise to any ifs, ands or buts at all. How much we humans do love certainty.

"Soon you'll be able to send your future partner to a psychologist in the Department of Love, and instead of spending years of arduous letter writing and mutual visits, you read each other's accurately outlined profile and you know: there is no possible error here."

"Now you've lost it completely," Marion says. "I think you need a study break." And, undeterred, she continues sucking pretty sentences for Peter from her much-used fountain pen.

At first, two or three spots appeared below the left corner of her mouth, then five or six above it, another two to the left of them. Now it is a little assembly that is creeping toward the first spots and beyond, and down her chin all the way to its farthest point. Now the battalion makes an about-face— because, by now, it's a regular battalion—toward the right with full marching power: it's just a matter of a few days now until Gorda's face is completely covered in spots, no, little hills, tiny mountains. Taken aback, Gorda stands in front of the mirror and squeezes, without success, this or that protruding spot. No, clearly, they are not pimples. Pimples can be opened and closed and, finally, they just disappear. These growths, however, show no entryway and no possibility of evasion. This is worse than facial hair, Gorda thinks. I'd rather have thick facial hair than such a face in my face. Slippers with fur trim are nothing in comparison! How am I supposed to visit Remo in the spring now? "Oh, the rat," Gorda whispers, the rat, and she lies down in bed: she, the mountains in her face, and the rat. Until only the rat is still lying there.

"Marion, come and help me. I'm turning into a moonscape." Marion immediately stops sucking beautiful sentences for Peter from her fountain pen. This is a genuine emergency. Because, perhaps, the mountains don't move from spot to spot but rather from face to face, and the next face in this room is Marion's. In any case, with such mountains around her mouth, she couldn't face Peter. If she looked like that, no one would ever reach out for her. No one would say: "Your beautiful voice" and mean: "Your beautiful skin." Never again will anyone protect you when he places his hand on you. What's the use of a beautiful soul and of beautiful sentences on paper if the packing is worn out—worn out thirty years too early.

"You've got to see a doctor right away," Marion says breathlessly because she just saw her own face full of mountains floating in the room.

"Is a doctor really able to move such mountains?" Gorda asks despondently. But if a doctor can't do it, who can?

"You're going to the dermatologist tomorrow," Marion says breathlessly.

———

The doctor looks baffled: well, what do we have here?

He squeezes and strokes. But squeezing and stroking don't achieve a thing. Gorda had tried that herself. To do that, he wouldn't have had to study for six or more years. Finally, he walks over to a cupboard, from which he takes a little vat with a white liquid.

"Put this on the warts," he says and names the malicious spots, which are no longer stationary mountains but are now something moving at a gallop.

At home, Gorda immediately smears the white liquid on her face. It shines like milk and singes like red coal, singes a big hole into her chin. And miraculously, new mountains rise up from the hole. To Gorda's and Marion's horror.

"You can't go to Bunten looking like this," Marion says, shaking her head and checks the area around her mouth every day for infection. Even though the doctor had said: "They are not contagious." And with a big hole in her chin, Gorda met Heinrich in town.

"Oops, what's that?" He asked with a look that said: I knew that you'll never be my type.

"Oh, nothing," Gorda mumbled although she knew: All is lost if I have to continue living with such a hole in my chin and the mountains on my cheekbones—because now they are also colonizing the cheekbones.

And Marion washes her hands when she touches Gorda's arm, and Marion washes her hands when she puts away Gorda's cup, and Marion washes her face whenever she looks in the mirror.

"But he said, they are not contagious," Gorda says too forcefully because she doesn't believe it anymore herself. "My girlfriend doesn't want to share the room with me any longer," Gorda tells the doctor in a sad voice. "Something's got to happen. The white liquid tears holes in my face but doesn't move any mountains."

"There's only one way out," the kind man says, gets a huge drill, and holds it above Gorda's face. Great, am I at the dentist?

"Move your chin up to me," he says to the fearful child, using the informal address. "It may leave a few scars behind."

Oh well, what are scars compared to a landscape of mountains and valleys. He drills over here and over there with needle pricks under her chin. Is he possibly planning on drilling all one hundred mountains? It lasts an eternity. This is how fear gives in: you just can't push the nail of your right thumb into the palm of your right hand for three hours just to drown out one pain with another. Just to be the creator of your own pain?

"But child," the doctor says. "What have you done with your hand?" And he lays the drill back onto the table. "All right, this will do for today. Come back in a week: We'll see who is going to win this."

In the course of the next night, the battalions around the right corner of her mouth retreated. There had, however, only been one little prick. The electric needle accomplished in three seconds everything that all her scratching and squeezing over the past weeks hadn't been able to do: it dealt a devastating blow. Twenty-four hours later, the troops around the left corner of her mouth and her chin had also packed up their belongings. Then the mountains on her cheekbones follow suit, as do individually scattered spots above the left side of her nose. The battlefield is being evacuated, the mountains moved and leveled. Her morning skin fresh as dew, Gorda looks forward to the sunny days in Bunten with a smile. But how easy is it to be transformed from a young girl into a wart witch, Gorda thinks and will never forget the days when her happiness hung by a fine needle.

"You see, child, we did win," the kind doctor says and looks at the tortured palm of her hand. "You downright shredded your skin. I've never seen anything like it."

And Marion continues to suck beautiful sentences for Peter from her fountain pen and doesn't have to wash her hands all the time. Yesterday, she even drank out of Gorda's mug.

———

With each day, Gorda looks more and more like Hermione. She sits with her back toward the window, bowed over hills of pages that are covered with numbers, and she follows direct mathematical paths that draw her closer to the secrets of intelligence and character. Tests must be be as short and succinct as possible so that no valuable time for designing the future will be lost. So this soul here has a clear drive toward profound issues such as exploring the linguistic features of a text, and the soul that artfully connects one number to the next will without doubt rise to be an excellent accountant. Yes, of course, of course.

With each day, Gorda longs more for the packaging of beautiful sentences. Sometimes she pores again over fanciful poems by Eichendorff instead of suffering clear graphs and irrefutable lists. Perhaps she'd rather stick with uncertainty and ambiguity and things that are difficult to prove? But you just can't always force the rudder of your life's ship back and forth. First, you turn southward, then you turn northwest and, finally, toward home. And at home they say: "Well, can't you make any decision at all?" Once you've gotten yourself into hot water, you've got to get yourself out again even if the water is teeming with nasty formulas and erasers.

It seems obvious that Marion isn't majoring in English but in letter writing. She never opens the textbook, so thoughtfully purchased at the beginning of the semester, without immediately starting to stare at the wall, where there are certainly neither German nor English sentences.

Why should it say "Do something" in English there?

Gorda excitedly performs calculations, while she sees Marion's studies going down the drain on a comfy old bed. I'd like to have it easy like that.

Doing nothing without the voice in my head.

Doing nothing without the rat in my bed.

Doing nothing without shame and disgrace while strolling in the afternoons along streets full of dirty snow.

These are all paths that lead to the amphitheaters and into a profession.

Bed and strolls lead nowhere. And Gorda chews on and swallows numbers and disgusting charts and statistical graphs that are curved in an outrageously beautiful manner.

I can't take watching Marion's decline any longer. And I have to take it three more weeks. So you sit in the library instead of in your corner of the room, and you calculate and draw graphs against the meaninglessness of thinking. What will happen with Marion if Peter leaves her? She'll never get her degree this way. Oh well, what does Marion concern me? Just stay focused on your math book and your final exams and your thesis, which you have to finish before the exams. What will happen to Marion if Peter leaves her?

"Hey, this summer semester I'm going to Hamburg where Peter's studying." Marion says. "Next year, my studies will begin for real." Then she won't need to suck so many beautiful sentences from her fountain pen, Gorda thinks. Then she'll find her way to the amphitheaters. Then nothing will happen to her if Peter leaves her. With relief, Gorda lowers the math book onto her lap: And I will go to Freiburg, where an excellent psychology department shines its bright light all around. People there are half a step closer to the secrets of intelligence and character than anyone else. And from there, it only takes a few hours on the train to Remo.

So the separation is a done deal: relieved Marion and Gorda drink friendship tea and light a peace candle and eat cheerfulness cookies. For a long time now, they haven't enjoyed being together this much because they won't be together anymore starting next month. With a sigh of relief, Marion departs and leaves behind a pile of old pages full of the most beautiful sentences for Peter. Why didn't she throw them away, Gorda thinks angrily. Do I have to be the guardian who protects the privacy of her letters? And she reaches for a page. It says: "There is nothing more important in the world for me, dear Peter, than my profession. I do not ever want to marry or have children without having a university degree first. Therefore, I spend all my time memorizing English idioms: *A stitch in time saves nine*, while Gorda writes letters, eats cookies, makes coffee, and dreams her time away. You understand that I have to get away from here."

———

Come to Bunten, Remo wrote, before your trip home. And Gorda carefully packs for Bunten: her prettiest sweater, her prettiest dress, her prettiest shoes. No longer in slippers with fur

84

trim, no, she will stand in dark blue pumps before his mother, in a blue-striped silk dress. This way, even willpower become flesh will soften and look her up and down with leniency.

The evening before her departure, Gorda sits down in front of the new sun lamp, which was a gift from her mother and which she has never used. After all, why not? Oh right, because of the hills on her face. Maybe, they will keep growing even more eagerly in the artificial sunlight, she had thought. I'd rather wait for a more convenient time. That more convenient time has come: her skin shines in a smooth and ailing pale manner in the light of the winter-gray snow sun. I'll now bring spring onto my cheeks and the red sky of the morning onto my forehead and skin. Gorda remains a little longer than suggested in front of the lamp so that its rosy effect might last a few days longer. Just an hour later, it seems like the heat of summer is burning on her skin.

The next morning, the burning sensation doesn't feel like summer anymore but full of deceit and malice, and the look into the mirror becomes a look into a volcano's abyss, into a bottomless pit that shoots with fire-red flames. Her skin screams bloody murder, what have you done to me? Oh, my God, I can't go to Bunten looking like this, Gorda thinks. I won't be able to withstand any willpower become flesh. And the worst is that not her whole face is in flames but for two white rings around her eyes, right where Gorda had placed the protective goggles. Now she looks white on red—no one would want to take that look to Bunten.

She takes her lipstick and paints flames around her eyes: Now her whole house is ablaze, and there is no hope for improvement over the next three days. The packed suitcase, however, wants to travel, and her heart seeks comfort in Remo's protective words on the phone at the train station: "That doesn't matter; just get on the train right now!"

Weak-willed, she boards the train. Remo gives her willpower. He willed it so. Now it is up to him to extinguish the whole-house fire with comforting outpourings of words. He laughs as he looks at a garish red Gorda at the Bunten train station and pushes her into the tram because she has no compulsion to move forward. If only she didn't immediately have to see the willpower become flesh but were able to bolt into her room with blue flower design right away. But, no, the willpower stands guard at the front door and denies her a cowardly escape. With zeal, Gorda explains her skin damage, and yet no explanation in the world helps if you're burned down with soot in your eyes when you step in front of your enemy.

"I've got to tell you something," and Remo is looking around as though looking for explanations. "I really could not have known before, so just don't threaten again to leave right away. You've got to meet him sometime. To make a long story short: my brother is in Bunten."

What? His brother from Bonn, the professor of German literature and substitute father—I'm supposed to come before him as a burning house, as a fire-spewing volcano, as burned-down ruins?

"I'm leaving immediately," Gorda says.

"You're not leaving," Remo says. "You're staying. Your red skin isn't really that red; it's just a little too red. What does your red skin matter to me anyway, as long as I love you? The only thing that matters is that I love you."

Yes, the only thing that matters is that Remo loves me. My red skin, my small mouth, my strong chin, everything, everything is nothing in the light of Remo's love—and he takes her into his arms: here everything is good and right and well-formed and healthy. "Just go and freshen up a bit now. I'll introduce you to him."

Remo has barely left the room, and nothing is good and right and well-formed and healthy anymore. I can freshen up as much as I want: No water in this world will extinguish this fire, no lipstick will cover up these white rings around my eyes. How happy I would be if I could meet him in fur-trimmed slippers and with my skin pale. Instead, I'll wear dark blue pumps and blue-striped silk, but a person's head is the most important thing about them—now, do tell: what does your head look like? If only I had left my head at home! But I've got to stick out my head and neck in front of his brother.

<hr>

And he looks amused or astounded or just indifferent— who can tell when you're looking inward out of fear at the thousand thoughts seething within you. Then Remo hands her a glass of wine, and she clinks glasses; whose glass she doesn't know. She drinks in a bit of calmness. Calmness, calmness, the only thing here that matters is Remo's love. And one more sip and another sip. And Remo keeps refilling as though he senses that he's serving calmness. And so, calmness spreads over her seething thoughts. And his brother is talking. He's been talking for a long while, but Gorda hasn't been able to pay attention for as long as her own thoughts were talking. Now, however, when there's calmness, now she listens, no, actually she still doesn't listen, she watches.

His brother must have a different father than Remo—a short, gentle, bespectacled intellectual father with a high forehead and blond locks of hair on his temples. Behind such a forehead, entire library halls certainly must reside. Everything there—book and shelf and catalogue—is well organized, that means, within reach at all times. In her case, books are thrown sloppily into her brain, and when she looks for a historical date, she never knows where it might be hiding. Remo's brother always knows where his knowledge is. He opens his mouth, and out comes the book he read most recently. Or is it his own book he is talking about? It sounds like a lecture in the amphitheaters, read from internal pages.

Remo keeps giggling during the lecture. The willpower become flesh smiles with pride. These are my dear sons, her glance says: We Ourselves, and we must stick together. And what keeps them together keeps you out. Remo giggles and giggles. It's not even Remo, it's the wine. No, not the wine, it's the rat. Oh my god, the rat. How it giggles away in my brain!

"You just drank too much," Remo says to Gorda as she lies in bed with the pillow over her head and earplugs in her ears.

"No, it is the rat," Gorda whispers. "Don't talk so loud, you'll wake it up again."

Remo's brother, whose name is Jean, not Hans but Jean because the influence of French shows in every nook and cranny of Bunten—so you don't say 'cold cuts' but 'charcuterie'— anyway, next to Remo, Jean looks like a gentle librarian next to a hero from Swiss prehistory. Jean has these long and thin fingers that so expertly turn pages, he has this glassy and polished glance that doesn't want to look up even after reading a hundred pages, he has these skinny arms that are only able to carry one book or perhaps two at the same time, and he has the mighty head to go with his inconspicuous systems for digestion and locomotion that are, as by some miracle, typical of most intellectuals. Remo, in contrast, has the body of a sword-carrying he-man, the swashbuckling horseman. You'd perhaps see them together depicted as *vita activa* and *vita contemplativa* on old drawings.

Gorda had seen such a drawing hanging in the Tübingen library. And now stands before a living pair of contrasts that, however, doesn't want to form any contrasts because Remo wants to be like his brother: his strong shoulders and arms are not to pick up a sword or a crossbow, but perhaps two or three books for reading. His gorgeous and narrow-hipped body with its strong and well-formed legs is not to ride a horse or sit in a racecar but to gingerly walk back and forth between rows of books. And his heroic head with its black curls is to disappear, covered in dust, into the twilight of inner rooms. What a shame, Gorda thinks, that Remo wasn't born a few hundred years ago. At that time, skinny Jean would have needed his brother's protection. Yes, he would have honored and admired him as his role model and savior: Oh, Remo, if only I had arms as noble as yours, if only I could ride as elegantly across the battlefield, if only I spied with eagle eyes from the ramparts, instead of frittering my life away by reading in darkened rooms.

Vita activa and vita complativa, frontispiece to Vita S. Norberti's
Patriarchae Antverpiae Apostoli

Those are times long gone—*Tempi passati*!

Now it's Remo, who curses his eyes and weakens his eyes and allows his legs to wither in libraries. And who giggles with approval in front of his brother when he should not be giggling but laughing. This giggling that does not suit such a strong man.

Finally, Gorda pays attention to what Jean is saying: "Remo, Justi sends her best wishes, really her best, I tell you. How pretty she looks. A pretty *meidschi*."

So, best wishes for Remo from a pretty girl, a pretty *meidschi*. Sends her best. And Remo's own brother is the messenger for these best wishes. And I don't exist here at all while Jean looks at his brother as though he wanted to whisk him away with magic. Whisk him away from me.

"Who is this Justi?" Gorda asks in the room with the blue flower design. And Remo laughs—yes, he laughs and doesn't giggle when he's with her.

"Oh, forget it, my brother just likes her."

"He doesn't like her for himself, he likes her for you, Remo. And why does he like a woman for you. A pretty *meidschi*, and I don't exist here at all!"

"Don't be so sensitive all the time," Remo says. "What does good old Justi matter anyway. What matters is my love."

Good old Justi, Gorda thinks. When will there be a good old Gorda?

"Are you going to start with Justi again," Remo says. And spears a disgusting snail with his fork while Gorda is poking at her ragout. "Just stop. She's irrelevant to me. Believe me."

"But she's not irrelevant to your brother. He likes her, and he doesn't like me. And I don't want to be with a brother who doesn't like me."

"The only thing that matters is that I love you," Remo says, and his eyebrows tighten like two menacing beams while his mouth smiles, smiles in vain.

And then they take a stroll under the colonnades of the city's Middle Ages.

"This clock here," Remo says, "is about four hundred years old."

The four-hundred-year-old clock shines in fresh colors and its precious old hands are made of carved iron, and I'd be able to enjoy everything if there were no Justi, no brother, no willpower become flesh.

"Well, look who's there," Remo says, and Gorda doesn't understand any of it because he speaks dialect and not standard German. In an automatic reflex, Gorda shakes hands obediently and, with an angry glance, obediently watches: how a girl makes moon eyes at Remo, gazing upward from below because she is much shorter than Remo while Gorda—inconvenient for making moon eyes—Gorda is as tall as his forehead. The girl has a smooth, round face. You would call it "nice" if she just stopped overdoing it with her eyes wide open and moist lips. I mean Remo isn't all that handsome. And this adoring gaze with moon eyes doesn't come from nothing. It is a way of talking and has the brother's approval; otherwise, she wouldn't declare in a loud voice: "You and I, we should soon go for a stroll." And Remo giggles. The same giggling as with his brother, and it agrees with Justi: Yes, we should soon go for a stroll. Pretty

Remo and Gorda

soon, I'll have had enough, Gorda thinks. She feels the burning sensation on her forehead and in her stomach.

"Now come, we've got to go," she says brusquely and directs the adoring girl's eyes to her red skin. Suddenly, they are no longer adoring but now size up the strange natural phenomenon: That's supposed to be my rival?

Good, I know, I'm nobody's rival today, and now I will just go away. Away from the giggling, from wide-open eyes, from the incomprehensible dialect, and from comprehensible sorrow.

"Tell me what came over you to just walk off like that," Remo says next to her in the colonnades. "Am I to blame if we run into Justi? Do you think I had planned the meeting?"

No, it was your brother who planned it, but that's almost just as bad.

"Justi, Justi, what kind of crazy name is that anyway?"

All worked up, Gorda paces back and forth in the room with the blue flower design and completely forgets that Gorda means "the fat one" in Spanish and is a crazy name for the slim German girl that she is. Finally, Remo's eyebrows and mouth are smiling simultaneously. "Her actual name isn't Justi; it's Justitia."

"How can you name your daughter Justitia?"

With zeal, Gorda shifts to attacking the parents.

"It's not just the daughter and her name that are crazy, but so are her parents and grandparents and great-grandparents."

There's a story behind it, and Remo giggles to himself as though he were with his brother: "Justi's mother lived in an apartment with view of the Fountain of Justice for years. And so her father didn't fall in love only with her mother but also with the statue on that fountain," he says. "And later he named his daughter after the statue." "And his son is probably named 'Child-Eater,'" Gorda says angrily because Bunten has a hideously beautiful fountain on which a Swiss cannibal devours babies, he's got one right in his mouth and the second one in his arms. That is how Bunten warns its children: Watch out, or the child-eater will get you!

"No, his name is Rudolph. However, we have a monument to Rudolph von Erlach here, but that's certainly a coincidence."

"And what does Justi's father, this Gordon, do when he's not naming his children for stone figures?"

"He's a law professor, a boringly normal law professor."

And never again will Gorda walk past the Fountain of Justice without thinking about Justi or past the Child-Eater Fountain or the Fountain of Virtue, from which a skinny female figurine beckons to practice temperance and still is reminiscent of the buxom Justitia, because the same stone carver made them. That's how every square in the city warns or recalls or threatens or praises some idea turned to stone.

"These fountains were the meeting places of the Middle Ages," Remo explains. "That's why there are so many of them here. Back then, the people stood below a daily moralizing sermon made of sandstone, at whose feet water babbled, so that they wouldn't get any feverish ideas. And what newspaper and radio are today was then the enjoyable gossip at the fountains."

And for me every single fountain turns into Justi. How can I be happy in a city where my rival lurks around every corner? Yet there are not only alarming fountain figurines in these untouched Middle Ages, but there are also thousands of tiny painted heads that stare down from cornices and entryways. Whenever you look up, you see a whimsical or tense or sneering old man's face. Were these old men supposed to keep the women of the city in check? Gorda thinks in disgust. Young men, after all, won't be scared by geezers. They will still do what they want to do, unimpressed by either Child-Eater Fountain or Temperance figurine. It's always the women who hurry through life with hanging lips and sunken shoulders and fear of men in their stomachs. And from all the walls in the city, the evil eye is watching attentively.

The freshly painted clock of the tower, under which we met Justi, is the city's landmark. Yet there's not just this tower and this clock, there are towers all over the city center. And not one is without a clock that has pictures to tell of heroic battles by Swiss mercenaries against their murderous surroundings. Life is a battle, the clocks say. Life is short, say the clocks. You must always know which clock has struck the hour, say the people of Bunten. Clocks have eyes. Clocks have ears. They are watching you just as do the infuriating old-men faces. You won't get any feverish ideas if you see how, street by street, time passes rapidly.

On Hotel Street, it was 2:30 p.m.; on Goods Street, it's already five minutes past three; and on Chute Street, the knowing clock announces that it's late afternoon.

"Gorda, we need to go home," Remo says. "It's already six o'clock. My mother is waiting for us with dinner."

Maybe your mother is waiting with dinner for you. But she isn't waiting for me. She's more likely to wait for my departure.

So, she finally does take the train home just as her skin has changed back from salmon to beige silk. But how does beige silk in my face do any good when I'm on the train to Oldenburg?

"The only thing that matters is that I love you," Remo said when they said farewell. Gorda takes his signet ring from her purse, where she had kept it hidden in Bunten. She wasn't allowed to wear it there.

"You know, that would make my mother angry," Remo decided. "Certainly, you understand this. But here you've got me." Now she has the ring but not Remo. And the memories from the room with the blue flower design. She prefers not the think about the memories from outside that room.

"If they treat you badly there, just don't go there again," Mom says. "My dear child, nobody forces you."

"Maybe they don't treat me badly at all," Gorda says. "Maybe I'm hyper-sensitive. Maybe his brother doesn't want to set Justi up with Remo. Maybe I'm crazy."

"You're right. Maybe you're crazy," Mom says. Better crazy than not being allowed to see Remo again.

In the afternoon, Gorda looks at her suitcase and takes out the stationary pad that Remo gave to her with the words: "Don't forget to write me as soon as you get to Oldenburg." And now she holds his stationary pad in her hands in the way she holds his ring as though a piece of his love were glued to it.

"Remo," she whispers, "Remo," and lifts the paper to her lips. At that moment, she notices that the top sheet of paper must have served as a pad for writing. She clearly recognizes his handwriting. So clearly as though she were looking at a letter from him.

And she reads: "Dear Jean, I met with Justi last week just as you had wanted me to. It was very nice, but …"

"But-what-but-what!" Gorda yells because the indentation on the paper is masked by a second indentation. But only too briefly, perhaps. Now her unwanted tears gush forth. No tears! You want to meet with Cornelia this evening, and would you be able to do that with puffy eyelids. But the crying and sobbing of her pain brings back the memory of Justi under Bunten's landmark. Now she knows what's up, now she understands why Justi made those ridiculous moon eyes gazing upward, why she had her eyes wide open, and why she was wooing with her lips. Her glance didn't say: "we should go for a stroll soon," but it said: "we should go for a stroll soon again." And she was entitled to that glance, she was entitled to make moon eyes. Remo and his brother gave her that entitlement. And perhaps they are, just now, taking a stroll along the riverbanks, where we also took a stroll. And he explains to her why I visited him: Oh well, good old Gorda, she just stopped by. And I, the idiot I am, sit here and believed his ring in my hand. There is this shuffling of a couple of feet on the top left side. Stop crying, Gorda orders, you've got to accept it. The rat bites into Gorda's flesh. *Break up with him right away*, the rat says. And she goes to the telephone and dials his number, the only number she knows by heart.

"Remo, Remo," she whispers.

"Yes, what's wrong?" He says surprised. "Yes, what's going on? Why are you crying?"

"Justi," Gorda sobs. "You went out with Justi?"

"No, I didn't," Remo says.

"Yes, you did," Gorda yells. "I read it on your writing pad."

"Oh, that's what you're talking about," Remo says. "That was a courtesy meeting that doesn't mean a thing. The only thing that matters is our love."

"No!" Gorda shouts and slams the receiver down, where Mom grabs it and carefully places it back on the phone.

"What's going on?" She asks startled by such great grief. "Did something happen to Remo?"

"No, something happened to me," Gorda says, bawling.

It's over forever, the rat says and keeps biting at Gorda's brain.

"Just calm down," Mom says.

You'll never see ever him again, the rat says.

"You can think everything over," Mom suggests.

You saw it with your own eyes, the rat says.

"Just have a sip of brandy to help you calm down," and Mom returns with the bottle.

I don't want to calm down, the rat whistles.

Mom brings the pills and the ear plugs and the blindfold to Gorda's bed and decides: "Everything will certainly look different tomorrow."

She wakes up at three o'clock in the morning. The rat is biting, the rat is gnawing. She takes two more pills. Where's the stationary pad again? Here it is. She moves it under the light and holds it at a slant, this way and that, and she suddenly sees words where before tangled lines were running into each other. There she reads: But her cute manner ...

The rat bites down with renewed strength.

Oh God, she has cute manners. What's to become of me? But her cute manner—and what and what? There is something else coming, isn't there? But her cute manner has always irritated me, Gorda reads loud and clear. It irritates him, it says, and not the opposite as Gorda had expected.

But her cute manner has always irritated me: This sentence is the world's strongest happy pill.

After nine hours, Gorda wakes up, singing with happiness. Her cute manner has always irritated him, she hums the entire morning. The rat—gone. The evil voice on the top left side— gone. I'm allowed to see my Remo again. What are willpower become flesh, a match-making brother and Justi in light of this happy pill!

It protects me from the evil eyes of the tiny men on the cornices, it protects me from Justi's high bosom and her moist lips, it protects me from myself: from the feeling that I've perhaps been going mad.

In the evening, Remo calls her: "Everything's good again," she says. "I was able to finish reading the sentence."

"But what would've happened, if you hadn't been able to finish reading the sentence," he asks with apprehension in his voice. "I mean, what would happen, if I actually did, it could happen after all, even if it didn't mean a thing, I just want to say that life isn't ordered in an easy way. Don't get mad at me, but don't you react too strongly to every single little thing?"

Perhaps, you are crazy, he wants to say. Perhaps, I'll cheat on you for real tomorrow, he wants to say. And what kind of scene will you make then, he wants to say. Then I won't be at liberty to do what I want to do, he wants to say: Is she the right woman for me?

So, he plans to cheat on me. Didn't his father cheat on his mother? Didn't he tell me about a scene with his mother when she found lipstick on his handkerchief again and a rendezvous note in his pants pocket? Didn't he find this terribly funny rather than sad? Wasn't he the son of his dead father both in looks and spirit? Didn't his mother say: "He is exactly like my husband, and Jean is like my younger brother, who died of pneumonia." And how can I stand it if Remo meets with someone like Justi whose manner he likes just as much as my manner? I'd rather not want to have to cut that kind of cancer from my heart.

"You don't mean that for real," Cornelia says. "You might as well join a convent right away."

I must've been crazy not to stay in Tübingen. There I knew the library, the amphitheaters, every café and the students in them. During the winter, I could've looked for a nice room, but now I sit in a shabby hotel room in Freiburg all alone and have to find accommodations helter-skelter. Oh my God, and everything to be closer to Remo by three hours on the train. Although I so like travelling by train.

She looked for a room all day long, looking in vain. They were either storage rooms or already rented out. If she had known that Freiburg was famous for its student-housing shortage, then not even six trains would've been able to get her here.

Why does good luck so often show up in shabby disguises and, only as a memory, throws off the rags to appear in all its glory? In the glow of the evening candles with cookies and Marion's friendship tea. Who cares if she sucked sentences for Peter from her quill every day. Who cares if she didn't find her way to the amphitheaters. But she did not comfort me when the willpower become flesh ignored me and when the match-making brother talked about Justi. And didn't I often go to the library specifically because Marion stayed in her bed? And didn't I study so diligently because Marion postponed studying? How will I find the strength to get up in the mornings if I can no longer wonder about her?

And Gorda, in desperation, sucks her fountain pen, and do you remember, she writes, how we spent the summer lying on the meadows behind the house? I wish I were lying there right now and not here. Believe me.

At three o'clock in the afternoon, she signs the contract with the landlady, who gives her a six-page list of house rules to read. I don't care about rules. The main thing is having a roof over my head and a bed. And it isn't more than a dark cubbyhole with a bed and a tiny desk but coupled with the promise of getting the sunroom next door next semester, where a female medical student lives right now. A medical student? A future girl friend, Gorda thinks, and she can't wait for her to return from her summer vacation.

A few days later, Gorda hears stomping and hacking sounds. Well, what's that, is somebody limping? Or is somebody pounding a stick against the wall? When the door to the room next door opens, Gorda opens her door, as if by accident. What she sees first is a leg in a long plaster cast that reaches well above the knee.

"Hi," the medical student says, "I'm Karin Haller."

"What happened with your leg?" Gorda asks with interest.

"I broke my leg while on ski vacation, an unfortunate break, and now I'll be limping my way to university for weeks."

"I could help with your shopping?"

"Thank you so much, and just call me Karin, and let's use the informal form of 'you'—that just saves time."

Never before has Gorda more enjoyed being on a first-name basis.

Why don't you love a city that you don't know? And will fall in love with it within three months. The towers with its brightly painted clocks are reminiscent of Bunten, there are even colonnades here, although not as many as there. However, when you stand in Goods Street and look toward Michaelis Square, you think: Bunten. And when you walk through three more streets, what do you think? Tübingen. And after three months, I did love Tübingen. But not on the first day.

On the first day, you think: Why didn't I stay home? Now I have to take unfamiliar streets to unfamiliar libraries and to unfamiliar amphitheaters, drink in warmth and comfort in unfamiliar cafés, do my shopping in unfamiliar shops, and line up in the cafeteria with unfamiliar students. Everywhere I look: it is unfamiliar. Only the rolls and the strawberry jam in the mornings remind me of home, on the walls the three prints that I already had in Tübingen, and the slices of bread with tea sausage in the evenings. But how long does it take to chew two slices of bread with tea sausage? And right after that: a hole opens up. No, a tunnel. And you've got to get through that tunnel. At the end of the tunnel, there are friendships and dinners for two and a love of Freiburg. Yet what if there isn't a tunnel but just a hole that threatens with nothing but unfamiliarity in the end. And certainly you would love the city on the first day if you were only passing through or visiting for a week.

But I don't like living here.

Just three days later, she hurries in good spirits to the shops to buy food for two after her visits to the library and amphitheaters. Carrying the heavy bags doesn't matter to her: She does know after eating the bread with tea sausage, there will be no hole but a long conversation with Karin about this and that.

Karin talks about her medical studies, which would not be something for Gorda.

"Cutting open corpses and always looking at the wounds of sick people, that would depress me," she says.

"It depresses me, too," Karin says, and she looks depressed.

"Why don't you change your major?"

"It's too late," Karin says. "I've already completed three years, and I can't tell my parents that I'm studying something else."

"Just try it," Gorda says, and Karin looks even more depressed.

"I already tried. It's useless. My father would've liked to be a doctor, you know. He only sees the white coat of prestige, my daughter the doctor, and all that nonsense. He also believes being a doctor protects from illness: he suffers from a bad eczema, you know. 'You shall not suffer the way I do,' he always says as if I couldn't get sick as a doctor." And Karin looks depressed at a future with eczema.

She can't sleep at night. Her blue eyes rest above black crescent-shaped shadows. They make her look old.

"If I just could get married, I'd drop out of university."

"But Karin," Gorda says, "marrying doesn't protect you from illness."

"But from loneliness." And Gorda senses how lonely Karin had been during all of last year. Lying awake and alone every single night. Just as lonely as Gorda was during her first days in Freiburg. But at night, at least, she was as good as home in her sleep.

Whoever has no home searches for one. Even if it is a hole of a room with a lightless view of a wall of a house. The neighbor in the next room takes the place of your family and all your friends. In Tübingen, Marion was your home, and now it is Karin. And tomorrow, you hope, it will be Remo. Remo, who will take you in his arms and who will never let you return to your loneliness. Who understands that you need a home because you've lost yours forever. For who can return if you've once left? Only a loser does that. The winner stays away because he has won a wife and a job and an apartment. I now understand why Marion kept sucking sentences for Peter out of her fountain pen. She was so shocked by the thought of having lost her home forever. Now she needed a new home, and that was to be with Peter. And then she would be able to finally begin with her studies. Karin is also looking for a home to find the strength for the studies she doesn't enjoy and to sleep well at night instead of brooding: Will I ever find a home again? And didn't Cornelia write: "When I walk home from the library in the evening, I always glance into the well-lit rooms and see families sitting around the dinner table. You can't imagine how much I long to have a family of my own in these moments. At that point, I'm ready to drop out of university and just get married. But, of course, I know that's not possible ..." And hasn't Susette gotten married in the meantime and is expecting a child, like Marion wrote. Susette hadn't been able to deal with life without home at all. All her frills and bows meant just one thing: I'm looking for a new home. What looked like flirtatiousness was really a cry of desperation.

Remo, on the other hand, never lost his home because he left for just a short time and now is attending university in Bunten again. The house where he lives is his paternal home, and he will stay there forever. There's no doubt at all that he feels like the co-owner of his mother's apartment. I, however, have been only a guest at my parent's place. Even if I didn't know that before. Therefore, I need a home while Remo doesn't. The home that Remo could provide me with is the home of his mother. And his brother also feels at home there. But neither his brother nor his mother want me there. So how can I find a home with Remo? What's left are his loving arms and the room with the blue flower design. And I'd rather not think, because thinking requires making decisions. I'd rather keep writing letters, touching his ring, and take refuge in sleep as if it were home.

Yet the unwanted guests—the thoughts—show up, too, in the amphitheaters, in the cafés, and in the library: Remo is never lonely in the way you are. After all, he has his mother, and his brother often visits with his whole family. His old friends from school live in Bunten, and he even joined a fraternity. There are friends everywhere. And I have no one except for Karin. And even Karin I won't have for long because she wants to move back to her parents' city so that she won't be so lonely when she lies awake at night. Although Remo writes, I long for you all the time, he just can't long for her as much as she longs for him: Whoever has no home, longs the most.

Why does she think she has to be courageous and brave and conquer new university towns instead of being relaxed and rush through familiar streets? Why does she waste her strength with feelings of freedom and searching for rooms and trying out shops? Because she believes: That's what you do. Hasn't Max changed universities a couple of times, and isn't Cornelia talking about Kiel, where famous sailboat races warm the hearts, and about Munich, where Professor Weinrich teaches? And Marion always wanted to leave: "Well, in Hamburg, I'll begin my studies for real." And Hermione had set her mind on Erlangen ("they have an excellent math department there"). And wasn't Freiburg famous for its psychology department and its beautiful, slightly mountainous surroundings? Wasn't the carefree life of students also meant to be a kind of journey through Germany? And when you're twenty-seven or twenty-eight, you don't just have a job in the bag but you've also seen half the country. Only cowards never leave their comfy home. Only overachievers plan on getting their degrees in the shortest time possible. Of course, it takes a great deal of time if going to university also means going on a journey. Whatever you can accomplish during five years in one place will take you seven in two more places. Each transfer to another university means one more year, that's the conventional wisdom among students.

And yet Gorda envies Remo who hasn't laid out his studies as a journey, who never has to look for shabby holes of rooms and sits on the shady side of the house. Who won't expend any effort on feeling alienated and looking for friends, but who calmly and steadily revises his dissertation, which is growing by the week. Who doesn't do any shopping or wash laundry or follow twenty house rules because the landlady is his mother and because he owns a good part of the house himself. The Swiss legal code clearly states: Children inherit more than their widowed mother. So, in a technical sense, Remo rents out to his mother and not the mother to him. Remo's gait and Remo's voice and Remo's glance express: All of this is mine. Because it comes from my father. My father bequeathed this desk to me and this signet ring and this antique clock on the mantlepiece. Gorda, on the other hand, owns three prints on the wall, two wool blankets, four sweaters, three skirts, a couple of pairs of pants, her overcoat, and one-and-a-half Sunday dresses. The money that's left after each month's fixed costs is just enough for the most essential things. And a glass of cheap wine before falling asleep at night. No wonder that Remo goes through the many weeks they are apart in a spoiled and patient manner while she feels alone and anxious about the future. What else, except for his doctoral degree, has Remo left to gain that he doesn't already have? But she has everything to gain: a degree and a new home and Remo, who does seem to long for her, but more like a rich man longs for another piece of property—patiently, cautiously, suspiciously, contentedly.

<hr>

However did I end up studying math, although it's officially called studying psychology? Did I really want to calculate formulas on a daily basis and set up lists and verify charts even if they say that is how I inch, one step at a time, closer to the secrets of the soul? Isn't this path to the soul a path to a smoothly running machine? And do we really have a machine-like character? A machine-like character and a machine-like reactive manner? I react to the most diverse situations by brooding—at times, leaning toward a "yes"; at other times, toward a "no." How can you account for a brooding nature like mine with yes and no? I would have to write an essay after each question on a test. For example, it says here: Do you always cross the street when the light is green? Of course, I often cross the street when the light's green, but not always. Still, more often yes than no. And if no, then I have reasons that seem more important to me than the rule of green. Sometimes I don't even have a reason other than wanting to do what I want to do. You're supposed to answer quickly in order to remain spontaneously and honestly on task. Spontaneous is not always honest. I have lied spontaneously in the past. On the other hand, I've also been honest after much brooding, even though spontaneously is not honest. These tests are made for simple souls. Do you really want to account for simple souls with simple questions or to anger complicated souls with simple questions? Is this question that stupid or am I not getting it? Again, Gorda seeks refuge in the libraries with novels like Fontane's *Effi Briest* and Keller's *Green Henry* because each sentence in them seems to hold more soul than the entire psychology curriculum.

"Go back to majoring in German literature," Karin suggests.

"But you got to finish what you started," Dad had said. "You already changed your major once."

Maybe I'm just a coward and don't want to walk to the end of the path I started. Because there's joy at the beginning and exams at the end. Even Remo prefers writing new pages each day rather than thinking about any concluding sentences.

"I still need to take a couple of preparatory courses for the exam," he says, "otherwise I won't pass the orals."

This way, he can take prep courses for years. In the amphitheaters, no one checks whether you are there. I'm not being missed here, you think, and then you'd rather stay away. But when you have stayed away, you know: Just today the meaning of my studies would have revealed itself. And now I sit here and have no idea at all what the whole thing is meant to be. So you prefer to attend. Yet, again, the meaning of your studies won't be revealed. Be patient: certainly tomorrow will be the day, or the day after tomorrow or the day after that. You can't be a student without studying, after all. So learn these formulas by heart even though they appear to be incomprehensible. Or inappropriate. Or ridiculous. Or crazy. After all, it hasn't been decided by a long shot who's the crazy one here.

———

This time, she has shoes on her feet and not slippers. This time, her face is ivory colored and not burnt red. This time, she knows whom she is about to meet in Bunten: Jean's English wife and their little daughter Lizzy. Still, Gorda is afraid because she's always afraid when she thinks about "we Ourselves." More people who consider the apartment their own, more enemies who want to keep Remo for themselves. But a child can't be your enemy, my God, Gorda. That's how crazy you've already become.

Jean's wife Betty is tall and delicate and has long delicate curls like a twenty-year-old although she's in her thirties. Her skin is so delicate that it takes on a reddish hue when she drinks red wine as if it had been discolored by it. It looks pretty. Her voice is high and clear and friendly even though she doesn't speak in a particularly friendly manner to Gorda. It is as though you had told a friendly person: Don't be friendly to that person. She doesn't belong to us. And now she just obeys. But the child is still at an age where they tell the truth, and you just cannot tell her anything without her blurting it out. She associates Gorda with we Ourselves, whether they want that or not. For the child, Gorda is a play pal and a substitute aunt on whose lap she likes to sit. The grandmother smiles with a face like a mask: Lizzy never sits on her lap.

"I don't understand her," Lizzy told Gorda. And then she told her a long story about kindergarten and her friend Tom. Mother Luck looks stern during dinner because now Betty also speaks in English riddles and Remo speaks in English riddles, while she can only say "please" and "sweetheart" and "I don't understand" in English. Gorda is not excluded any more, but Remo's mother is. Yet she doesn't accept this without contradicting, demanding they all speak German: "Hier wird nur Deutsch gesprochen!" That's how she stops the conversation and, suddenly, is able to say this in standard German and not just in Swiss German. But Lizzy insists on English. And they give her what she wants; otherwise, she'd throw a tantrum.

"My apologies," Betty says haltingly in German with her fine British accent. And keeps talking in English with Gorda because that's faster. Mother Luck sees that she's lost her family to Gorda for the moment. In spite of her warning: She is not one of us.

"Lizzy's definitely got to learn German," she orders. "It can't go on like this."

"She'll learn it in school anyway," Betty says. "We'll just have to wait another two years."

Two years seem too much for the grandmother, you can tell by her long face.

"Couldn't see attend a German kindergarten?" She asks, feigning surprise that this hasn't happened yet.

"She's still too young for this," Betty says. "I don't want to confuse her."

"Confuse her, that's ridiculous," Remo's mother says and now is really angry: "Children learn in their sleep."

"And unlearn in their sleep," Gorda responds, but she shouldn't have said it. Mother Luck shoots these she-is-not-one-of-us glances for the rest of the evening.

The child tore down the wall of silence. Betty, too, is not just reserved anymore as she sees how much Lizzy enjoys climbing up on Gorda's lap. In addition, Gorda is taking the child off her hands for a couple of days, and so Betty returns from her daily shopping in high spirits. And Remo laughs a lot

Profile of a Young Woman, oil painting by Gorda, after an original by
Antonio de Pollaiuolo, 1429-1498

now and doesn't giggle that often anymore because he sees that Gorda is contentedly playing with his niece. "She's really nice to Lizzy," she hears Mother Luck say on the phone, and she understands the sentence even though it is in Swiss German. To her own surprise, every so often, she understands a piece of this enigmatic language.

But she still cannot imitate it, nor does she want to.

They all can speak standard German when they want to.

But they just don't want to.

"You know we were forced to speak standard German in school," Remo tells her. "It was like having to learn a foreign language. And we fought against it as much as we could. Everybody who tried to speak standard German well was punished as an overachiever and show-off. So you just preferred not to speak standard German."

"And why do you speak it so well?" Gorda asks with interest.

"I dared to only in Bonn. In school I used to speak a kind of standard German that sounded like Swiss German. A kind of intermediate language. All Swiss do that."

"So they could speak better standard German if they wanted to," Gorda says indignantly. "I knew it."

"The Swiss feel humiliated when they speak standard German. You must understand that. It is as if the Germans were occupation forces, a linguistic occupation force. The French-speaking Swiss have no such problems. Their French is considered the best in the world."

"And students from all over the world come there to learn French, but no one comes to Zurich or Bunten?" Gorda asks amused.

"Oh, we still have enough international students." Remo's eyebrows firmly tighten to one beam. "But, in fact, none who wants to learn German here."

"God knows, people can't learn German here," Gorda says. "People learn here that they are not liked as Germans."

And she wishes she were able to speak French. Then she could hide her German ugliness behind this elegant wall of language, which all German-speaking Swiss admire and desire to learn. Every higher-class citizen of Bunten spends a year among the French-speaking Swiss. When Remo's father planned on marrying the beautiful farmer's girl Elsie, he immediately ordered her to take French lessons. No English but French lessons. And, indeed, Mother Luck is able to say whole sentences in the elegant language of the neighboring city, which lends a certain high-heeled feel to her speech. Swiss German, on the other hand, emanates more the feel of sensible orthopedic shoes. It's got to drive you to desperation: you speak a dialect that no one understands in any other country, not even in Germany.

That no one wants to understand. Just yesterday evening, we sat around the table and drank a glass of wine and a fruit schnaps and talked with each other, as poorly as that went. Today the living room has become a film room with chairs and arm chairs on one side and the film on the other. It shows us again and again how the young Kennedy was shot and how some war is being prepared, or is this already the real war? Every day, we inspect the violence in the most beautiful corners of the world and call it news. Whatever collides in Japan, whatever blows up in Vietnam, whatever is murdered in Africa. We take on the misery of the entire planet.

"Turn the TV off already," Betty says to Remo. "I don't want Lizzy to see these catastrophes."

But we remain spellbound by the catastrophes. Perhaps, they are happening right in front of our own door right now? We've got to know whether our own order will explode full force on TV tomorrow.

At night, Gorda dreams about skirmishes that may be the real war.

"Take Lizzy to bed when the news start," Remo says annoyed the next evening.

We've got to know what's going on. And so now we always know what's going on: and it's the most disgusting, the most cruel, and the most disturbing. It seems as though nothing else is going on. "Bloodthirsty like the Romans at gladiator fights," Betty says. And Lizzy goes to bed before the news. Right after fairy-tale time so that she gets a good sleep. But our sleep keeps getting worse.

The psychology department needs testing material for its upper-division students, and we lower-division students are the ideal material: free of charge, submissive, intimidated. Because those who protest might as well go to the cafés to dream their studies away. As future industrial psychologists, they of course want to know how it feels to be tested. Of course.

On the first day, the character test comes hailing down on Gorda with its trick question and its cross-referenced questions. With a speed that requires spontaneity. "Or superficiality,"

Gorda says. "Half the questions—I could've also answer with no, Karin."

"Then just write down 'yes and no,'" Karin thinks her answer is funny.

The aptitude test is really a joke: it had never heard of my aptitudes. Or I'd have to break out into dance. And draw a picture that would hit hard. Are these questions by chance meant to show my acting skills in the right test light? And there are no secrets of beautiful sentences for an industrial psychologist? That person only knows about sparse definitions.

The IQ test comes along in a military-athletic manner, with stopwatch and shouted orders: "Start, stop, start, stop!" Three minutes for this page, two-and-a-half minutes for that section, six minutes for the second part. Gorda needs the prescribed minutes to read the instructions. "Stop," the professor of industrial psychology yells before she got started. "Start," the professor of industrial psychology yells before she can finish.

I can't think if I have a stopwatch right in front of my eyes. I don't respond to orders.

Wasn't I just yesterday able to solve a tricky homework problem? The good ones go into the pot, the bad ones go into your crop. And whatever goes into the crop is not valued by anyone. I'm bad testing material. In the middle of the yell "Sta-art!" Gorda grabs her belongings and bolts into the redemptive noontime air.

Her heart, which used to beat without being the center of attention in any way, now refuses to do its natural job without a throbbing insistence on consideration. "Just imagine, Karin, when I was in town, I had to stop every few minutes because I felt such twinges in my chest."

"Go see a doctor," Karin suggests. "Or no, it's probably something that'll just go away." But it lingers on. So much so that Gorda doesn't want to go downtown anymore. Her heart hurts with every step. And her letters to Remo get shorter and shorter. At my age, I just can't write about pains in my heart. And, after all, they aren't simple heart issues. They are jumps of the heart. Start, stop, start, stop, her heart jumps in her chest.

And her heart jumps. In town, in the library, while shopping, in the psychology department. Gorda prefers to stay in bed and read. No more mathematical formulas and statistical curves, please. She puts her psychology book into the closet. She also always feels tired, too tired to write to Remo. What could she be writing to him anyway? There's absolutely nothing going on, all she does is lie in bed and sleep and read and sleep. You just can't write to anybody that you're too tired to get dressed, too tired to go downtown, too tired to go to the university. No one would believe it. Or people believe you, and that would be worse.

What's the purpose of your life anyway? Is it worthwhile to work for forty or more years for that little bit of food, clothing, and a roof over your bed? Shouldn't you rather just sleep them away right now?

Karin has already left town, but Gorda has to stay in Freiburg for twelve more days to wait for Remo. Then she'll meet him in Schaffhausen and go with him to Deutersheim.

For two weeks, she'll be there alone with him, that makes spending the days in Freiburg in bed worth it. She doesn't want to get up anyway. Getting up means your heart jumps. By the time I take the train to Deutersheim, those jumps have to be gone. Therefore, I'm recuperating in bed. That's the best place for this purpose. Still, she needs to go shopping once in a while. The whole rigmarole of getting dressed just to buy bread and cold cuts and a bottle of wine. Why do the people over there look at me strangely? Is something wrong with me? On the fifth day, she feels exhausted from loneliness. You just can't lie in bed and sleep and read all the time. So get dressed and go downtown. Downtown, she feels her heart jump and needs to rest in a café before she goes to the movies. In the movies, you forget who you are. That lasts for two hours, then you know who you are again. Starting with the eighth day, Gorda goes to the public pool early in the morning. There are the same families at the same spots every day. In front of me and to my left, there are always two young women with their children. And Gorda listens to their conversations as though she belonged to their group. As though she had a home and a family. The young blonde with glasses talks about Heinz all the time. Heinz repaired my armchair. Heinz ran late when he had to pick up our daughter from kindergarten. Heinz doesn't feel like visiting his parents this year. Gorda would likewise be able to say: Remo put up our new bookshelf, Remo repaired the kitchen faucet, Remo doesn't feel like calling his mother. Instead, Remo repairs his mother's armchair, puts up her bookshelves and types the bills for her. No one is typing or putting up or repairing anything for me.

In Schaffhausen, Remo picks her up at the train station with the old Volkswagen borrowed from his friend Volker. Alone in the car with Remo: As though you had a home. Tiredness, loneliness, the dark room in Freiburg, the blonde and her Heinz—everything, all of it, falls away from Gorda with a loud sigh of relief. "Why are you sighing like that?" Remo asks. "Don't you like it here?" And does she ever like it here! Yet she can't tell him: "I think two more weeks in Freiburg, and I would've died." Then she says it; however, in a way that sounds like a lie. "No one dies that easily," Remo says amused, and he doesn't know how easy it is to die when you're too tired to get up. And although she is now safe with him in the car and has a home, Freiburg will return in the fall. Freiburg—without Karin and with a menacing psychology department. Start, stop, start, stop, her heart jumps in her chest.

"What's going on?" Remo asks surprised.

"Oh, nothing," Gorda says. "I just have some weird pain here."

———

In Deutersheim, all windows offer a view of the Rhine and of Main Street. Remo's mother's house also looks out onto the Rhine in back and to the street in front, where once a handsome, young Swiss non-commissioned officer rode by on his horse and saw the young Elsie inside. That was a long time ago and the the non-commissioned officer is buried, as is the scandal and so is Elsie's great beauty. But Remo and I are alive and breathing and, at the moment, squinting our eyes in the blazing afternoon sun. And I'm allowed to spend two weeks here alone with Remo.

View from the Rhine bridge to the village of Deutersheim

"Well, not completely alone," Remo says worried. "My aunt lives downstairs, of course."

"Of course,"

"You'll see, she won't be in our way at all."

At that moment, Mother Luck's sister steps out through the door and is small and delicate and shy for kindness. There's no willpower become flesh, Gorda thinks, someone wants to be nice to you.

Remo's aunt takes the suitcase as if she were young and Gorda old.

"Please, no," Gorda calls out after her, "I can carry it myself." She probably carried her sister's suitcase just like that. And cleared away her dishes and been given her old clothes as hand-me-downs. Although this sister is the older one. But someone like Elsie is never the younger sister, she's always leading from the front and already has what she wants and gets even more.

The aunt stops with the suitcase at the top of the stairs. There is a home that opens up to Gorda's view. It is full of carpets and old furniture and too many pictures on the wall, it's more a kind of storage room for the apartment in Bunten ("we don't really have room for the old dresser, we'll take it to Deutersheim next time"). There's a room where you sleep and there's a room where you would cook if you could cook. For the first time Gorda thinks, it's a shame that I don't know how to cook. Although she always considered cooking a dumb art. But home-made meals are part of a home. Just like at her parents' home. And she hears her mother's voice: "If only I didn't have to cook all the time."

Unexpectedly, Remo's aunt stands in front of Gorda with a pot of vegetable soup. "I made it for you. You've got to be hungry." This way, Gorda has not only found a home but a luggage carrier, a cook, a good spirit. "I'm sure you want to be alone," the aunt says when Remo invites her to join them. Like a married couple, Gorda and Remo sit in their home and eat the hot stew spoonful by spoonful, and Remo opens a bottle of red wine and fills their glasses, and it's not wine that Remo is pouring, it's happiness.

Pure happiness.

The next morning, Gorda wakes up impatiently: "Let's go, I want to see the village." And you whistle in the shower although you can't whistle. And you slide into your clothes as if the devil were in hot pursuit—but, no, it's not the devil, it's pure delight and it pushes you forward faster than all the devils in the world. Remo can't find his shaving stuff and then he finds it after all. Gorda can't stand it in the stuffed apartment any longer. All of Mother Luck's apartments are so dark. Is that a coincidence? Let's just get out of here and into the morning light. She flies down the stairs because she's looking forward so much to the Rhine, which doesn't flow in its unwelcoming-majestic manner but is approachable as if it just were its own princely relative. At its banks, Gorda immediately takes her book out of her purse, as though a book were always a part of happiness, but she then sets it down to her left in the grass and looks out into the countryside that opens up on her right like a poem written in the air.

The village street is straight as an arrow and fairly broad, and Remo and Gorda are being peered at from many of the houses. They all once knew beautiful Elsie and the Swiss non-commissioned officer. That was a scandal back then—and now it isn't a scandal if beautiful Elsie's son walks along the street hand in hand with a person who's drifted by and lives with her in an apartment although the two aren't married. If anyone were to tell me today about Freiburg and my jumping heart, I would only be able to sing right into his face! And that although I can't even sing! But when I put on pants and a sweater in the morning, all I know about is delight and the Rhine and excursions around Lake Constance and bathing in the sun next to Remo's protective shoulders.

What does it concern me what blonde women say about their Heinz? I'd rather do my own talking and read to Remo from my nicely bound book, which is a present from him. I wrote the date into the book when I got the gift so that I'll never forget it: "See, this way there will always be another special August 20th."

And she never wants to forget that all the unhappiness and bad luck in the world float by, but the days of happiness remain chiseled into the heart. When, for example, did that horrible character test take place—she couldn't say. But it was on an August 14th that she met Remo in Schaffhausen, and it was on a July 30th when she met him for the first time in her life. On September 28th Remo celebrates his birthday, and on an August 22nd he gave her his mother's desk as a gift for a time when she isn't there anymore. And what does it matter that she's probably going to be there for a long while and that I don't even want the desk—there is now August 22nd, the day when Remo first spoke of a future in which only he and I exist and our desk and our bookshelves and our taste.

So it's worth being patient and and living for a future that's full of happy moments like the weeks here in Deutersheim. The extraordinary becomes a daily event. And Gorda doesn't want to live without such daily portions of happiness.

She actually wanted to take just a quick look at the thick red book, but in it there's a letter with Justi's name on it. Carefully, Gorda retrieves it from the book and pretends to go to the bathroom to be able to read it undisturbed. Remo is bound to call for her soon. The letter is from Jean, addressed to his mother. He writes that he first visited Justi's mother and then the Gordons in their lovely apartment, where his friend Herbert, the law professor, showed him the new rugs that his wife and he had brought back from a trip to Turkey. Well, isn't Justi's mother his wife, Gorda thinks confused. Or are they divorced? Why didn't Remo tell me?

As expected, Remo calls for her: "Honey, the rain just stopped. We can get going!" Yet it is raining now in Gorda's soul, such that she doesn't want to get going anymore: she only wants to know what's going on here.

Impatiently, she opens the door to the living room. "I found this letter in the book," she says without being ashamed for having read it. Remo should feel ashamed for having hidden the truth from her. "Why didn't you tell me that Justi's parents are divorced?" she asks in a menacing tone.

"But they aren't divorced. And why are you interested in this?"

"Here, read yourself," and Gorda flings the letter at him as if it were a disgusting snake.

With squinted eyes and narrow lips, Remo reads about Professor Gordon's new Turkish rugs. "That letter is really old," he says in a drawn-out manner as if the age of the letter would cancel out a possible divorce.

"Are they divorced or not," Gorda yells indignantly.

"Why do you always get so upset when Justi's name is mentioned in one way or another?" Remo pours himself a glass of wine although it's only three o'clock in the afternoon. There won't be a trip to the lake today. Whenever he starts drinking, it's the end of the trip for him. "There is a story," Remo says after the second glass of wine.

"So, a story," Gorda says mockingly. "Has yet another person been named after a stony figure?"

"No, not quite," Remo says and giggles as though he were standing before his brother. Gorda lights a candle.

"The story," she yells. "I want to hear the story."

"Yes, it's a real story," Remo mumbles in a pleasant tone as he pours his third glass.

"That's enough now. You're getting drunk at three in the afternoon."

"In vino veritas," Remo lectures. "You should've had that much Latin in school. Well, Professor Gordon, the law professor, had a client, a widow, whom he advised from time to time and who was certainly twenty years older than him and, therefore, not quite young, not quite young at all, I'd say. On the other hand, she was worth millions, which Professor Gordon regarded as absolutely indispensable for an aesthetically tolerable life, and he, too, wanted to be able to commit himself more freely to his studies of antiquity—at the time, he was writing a book on art in ancient Egypt, I think, on the art of cat depictions if I remember correctly. In any case, Mrs. Frankenbach's bank account replaced for him the freshness of youthful skin, at least for a while, I'd like to add by way of correction, because several years later, when he himself wasn't that young anymore, he fell in love with the wrinkleless skin of the wife of a philosophy professor and began an afternoon love affair that ended in her divorce and two children with Professor Gordon."

"So Justi is illegitimate?" Gorda asked surprised. "And what did Mrs. Gordon have to say about the bastards?"

"Oh, she has genuinely accepted them and allows them to visit her at her place. Justi calls her 'Aunt Emmi.' She has her own children from her first marriage, the wealthy Frankenbach brothers from Goods Street. Therefore, her husband has a right to have children, too, she once mentioned to Jean. And since she was too old to have his children, he just got them somewhere else."

"But her millions will remain with the Frankenbach brothers," Gorda says triumphantly as if Remo had speculated on getting the money.

"Of course," Remo says, and his eyebrows converge into one beam. "That's enough," he says and means it.

Oh, Lake Constance is gorgeous! A wide expanse like an ocean without a shore, and yet ringed by many shoreside towns that you can hurry through without a hurry and without a goal because you have arrived and never want to leave. Hills follow gently after the plains without any thought of mathematical formulas and torturous trick and cross-referenced questions to be answered spontaneously-dishonestly with yes or no. The only things that matter are Remo's shoulders, his relaxed lips and his calmly resting eyebrows when he drives with her along the Rhine and tells her about Elsie and the handsome Swiss non-commissioned officer and of deceased relatives who sometimes knock peacefully at dreams, but you never have to go and open the door for them. We're so well protected by the walls of the apartment and the kind invisibility of his aunt, who continually places soups and roasts and casseroles in their kitchen as though good fairies were cooking for us. This way there are no guilty feelings and no annoying gratitude. And her heart beats in an orderly and calming fashion when Remo says: "As far as I am concerned, you don't need to go to university. Do you think it matters to me whether you have a diploma or not? The only thing that counts is our love."

And Justitia is just some figure on a fountain in Bunten.

———

Even though Gorda now lives in Karin Haller's sunroom, there is no sun shining for her. For where there is no friendship, there is no sunshine. Why am I even alive, Gorda thinks and presses her hand against her jumping heart. Since she has returned to Freiburg, it has been jumping again. There may be orderly hours when she goes shopping and reads and drinks coffee, like everyone else. Yet going to the university becomes more breathtaking with every day. With every step she takes toward the university, her heart jumps in the opposite direction. I don't want to go there, her heart says and jumps. So

Gorda stays home while the meaning of mathematical formulas is being revealed to her fellow students at the university. The meaning of trick and cross-referenced questions. The meaning of life. And I just lie here and read Fontane's *Man of Honor* although long ago I've left behind me majoring in the secrets of beautiful sentences. I wish I'd gotten rid of the major in formulas and trick questions instead. But what would Dad and Mom say if I approached them with the words: "This major was a mistake." They would say: "Mistake or not, you've got to see it through to the bitter end, and that means the final exams for your degree." Start, stop, start, stop, her heart jumps in her chest. Gorda gives herself the order: Tomorrow, I will go to class. And the next morning, she once again doesn't even get up. And not the morning after that, either. Finally, scared, she hurries not to the university, but to the university doctor. He palpates her chest and her back, he touches and examines and doesn't say anything but: "Well, well, she feels a little lonely." Then he injects calmness of the heart into her veins. Now her heart jumps noticeably less. Or it jumps less because Gorda goes to class less.

Instead, she goes to Friedericke on Sunday, who lives close to the university and whom she had met in the doctor's waiting room. "Really, you're from Oldenburg," said the small round person with the thick golden glasses and the high bell-like voice. "I'm from the same area, from Leerheide." So Gorda takes a chance and tells her that she often feels lonely. And Friedericke looks in such a friendly manner through her unfriendly glasses that her narrow glances induce more calmness than the doctor's broad injections.

Now she visits Friedericke daily for tea. Until Friedericke says: "We could easily put another bed into this room." Gorda asks a fellow student from the trick and cross-referenced questions if she'd like to rent her room: "Yes, it is a room with sunshine, with good bus connections, and the landlady isn't able to monitor all of her twenty or more rules." A week later, Gorda packs her suitcase and two bags, takes the coziness-inducing prints off the moist walls and takes an expensive cab to Friedericke. Today, however, expensive is what fits the bill.

After breakfast with Friedericke, it's easy to take the three steps to go to class even though trick and cross-referenced questions threaten to be there. There also is a reading room, where you forget any compulsion to do math, because you know you're surrounded by the most beautiful books in the history of the world. Everyone here reads so peacefully as though the day had thirty hours, and there weren't any stopwatches anywhere. Friedericke is studying economics. "What a masculine major for such a feminine person," Gorda says. "How did you pick it?"

"My father also studied economics," Friedericke says. "I would've probably studied something else, otherwise. I would've liked to be a veterinarian, but my father thinks I'm too weak for that." Friedericke talks a lot about Rehtwinkel. That's a small town near Aachen, and it's the location of the only state-run commercial college, where you learn two years' worth of knowledge within one year, after you completed high school, of course. "And why did you go there," Gorda asks surprised. "After all, you wanted to attend university."

"Well, I didn't want to go to university, except for vet school or literature, maybe. So my father said, go to Rehtwinkel first and learn something that makes sense instead of learning silly things that you will later regret." In Rehtwinkel Friedericke put on weight where she didn't use to have any. "I have difficulties with my hormones, you know. That's why I went to see the doctor." But they had excellent food in Rehtwinkel, so Gorda doesn't know whether it was the hormones or the food.

"Let's buy a slice of cake," Gorda suggests and nervously feels her stomach, which is still flat. But flat for how long? A slice of cake every afternoon, and at five o'clock a visit by our new friend Botho from Sonnenweide. Friedericke also met him in the waiting room of the doctor who injects calmness even when Gorda no longer needed those injections. Botho, however, needs them in the form of small white pills that are meant to banish childish nightmares and profound memories.

He has quite a few of those to banish. Because his father was a rear admiral during the last war and his grandfather an admiral during the war before that. So there has been a military streak through three or more generations of his family. And, of course, both father and grandfather wanted to turn the children—Botho has three brothers—into efficient warriors for the next war. But strangely enough the Heavens had put an end to the militarism of the generation of the fathers, and the sons absolutely refused to stand to attention, march in rank and file, obey the drill whistle, and harbor brooding thoughts in their hard cots. This was obvious early in their childhood when the father, screaming and ordering around, forced his sons into the rightful life of a soldier, and the mother—"The weakness in the family must come from your side," his father had once yelled—always put extra pillows in their little beds, furtively gave them more food when their father ordered asceticism, and hid the drill whistle that the traitorous nanny, however, would find again on a regular basis. This went on until the mother whispered, "I'm leaving," and wasn't just threatening anymore. She meant it and left. With her the money left. The father was forced to sell the palace-like house, cancel the gardener, redirect the trips to Switzerland to neighboring Swabia. Only the traitorous nanny stayed on, but not forever. The frugal father eventually cut her position too and, with it, cut any feminine influence out of his life. This way, idle and in early retirement, he completely turned soldier and tutor and violent madman for four little motherless boys. No wonder that Botho has to take white pills that banish his memories.

Yet, obviously, the pills don't banish enough because Botho can't stop talking about his father. "We did well only when he wasn't there," he says while chewing cherry tart. "My grandmother had life handed to her on a golden platter. My mother's platter was silver. We brothers ate from our father's tin cups."

"Well, this plate doesn't look much like tin, does it," Friedericke says with kindness and offers him a second piece of cherry tart.

All three of them are trying to forget. Gorda her studies of trick and cross-referenced questions, Friedericke her missing out on an ideal course of study with cows, cats, and a gray northern sky. And Botho his father's tin cup. It's best to forget together. They plan a car trip to a well-known student restaurant in a wooded area. Botho's tiny car quickly fills up with three characters who are searching for forgetfulness, who just have to look at each other to break out into giggles of joy because they outwitted their studies today.

"So, why do you want to be a priest?" Gorda asks Botho a little brusquely, and she knows that she has no tact. But Botho also asked her why she always wears Remo's ring around her neck because that's just silly, and he asked Friedericke why she doesn't take off her glasses from time to time because they are definitely too thick. Since then Friedericke has been wearing sunglasses whenever possible. But Gorda keeps wearing Remo's ring.

"My father had decided that I was supposed to study law when he realized that I'm not cut out to be an admiral. So I studied law."

"And why aren't you studying law anymore?" Friedericke asks with her soft high voice that never sounds tactless.

"Because I wanted to be an actor."

"So, why didn't you become an actor?"

"I could not possibly tell my father, he would've killed me. So I said: actor or priest because I thought he would certainly go for actor."

"And how did your father react?"

"Law, he screamed, just law and nothing else. He didn't even take note of actor or priest. That day, I decided to become a priest."

"But do you really want to be a priest?" Friedericke asks gently.

"Do you think I would learn something horrid like Greek and Hebrew for any other reason?"

They all look in silence at the spruce forest to the left and right of them. Botho, however, has nothing of a priest about him.

"Actually, I already ought to be in the seminary," Botho says all of a sudden.

"What is a seminary?" Gorda asks warily.

"It means that I wouldn't be able to see you anymore."

"That is out of the question," Friedericke says, and her voice is just as brusque as Gorda's sometimes is. "You've got to postpone that."

Botho mumbles: "Let's talk about something else." And all three of them look at the nighttime world of fir trees as if there were something to see there.

"We're going to St. Ursel in the Black Forest in December," Mom yells into the wheezing apparatus. "We want you to come with us and also to invite Remo so that we can meet this miracle of a man."

"What?" Gorda asks incredulously. "You really want to, I've got to ask him … oh yes, that would be wonderful, I'm just surprised, oh, stop already." But Gorda is afraid he might say no. "I mean: If he lets himself be invited to St. Ursel for five days, then he is something like a son-in-law, and maybe he doesn't want to be a son-in-law? What do you think, Friedericke?"

"You've just got to see how he reacts. Then you'd also know more clearly where you stand. And you would like to know that."

Yes, Gorda would like to know that. "And if he does say no, what does that mean?"

134

"That still doesn't mean much," Friedericke says placatingly. But she can't do anything else but placate. Even if she also thinks that, yes, in that case he doesn't want to be a son-in-law. "My mother raised me to be a hypocrite," she calls it. With that she means her unwavering tact, her restive friendliness, which reach deep into her most secret thinking is, therefore, not hypocrisy at all but lived kindheartedness. Or does Friedericke intuit at times the fickleness of the human soul when she says: "They are really delightful people." I mean there just are not that many delightful people. That's why Friedericke refers to her tact as hypocrisy, although that means if you're sharp sighted to a normal degree, you should call out every little courtesy as a cunning lie. In any event, I prefer Friedericke's rules of decorum to the swords of truth of so many other people. I hope Remo is going to be hypocritical in the manner Friedericke is, even if he can't be honest this time.

"Would you like to come to the Black Forest with my parents and me? Oh, yes, really, I'm delighted. I look forward to it. They do want to invite you, pay for the hotel room and everything. That won't bother you? Oh, no, really not? I'm really delighted about it."

"He didn't even waver a second. What do you think that means?"

"First wait and see how they get along," Friedericke says gently. "And then take it from there."

"Oh, my God, I hadn't even thought of that. Of course: maybe they'll hate each other and no such thing as son-in-law and so on."

However, there's no trace of hate. Dad and Mom play the charming older friends and advisors. In the mornings, the four of them spend a long time at breakfast and discuss the excursions of the day. Remo laughs and doesn't giggle and tells entertaining stories about C. F. Meyer. Her parents never ask what he plans to do with his university degree, and they never ask about his plans concerning Gorda. So there's nothing about a son-in-law—and yet there's very much of it. Unspoken, for example, when Dad generously pays every bill, even though Remo says: "But no, you can't do that." Finally, Dad even suggests they be on a first-name basis. And as Remo addresses Dad and Mom using the German informal form of "you" for the first time, Gorda forgets all her worries about the future. And he's to come to Oldenburg over Christmas like a real son-in-law.

<hr>

"Oh, the wonderful strolls in the snow, Friedericke. They always made me feel so alive, even though I woke up every morning feeling like I got beaten up. I can't explain it. I'm just in my early twenties and I always feel old as dirt in the mornings. In the afternoon, I sink like my grandmother into my pillows. And when Remo comes to take me into his arms, I think, good God, I'm so tired. But, of course, he's not supposed to notice because who wants a young woman who is already seventy. I felt like I was hiding some kind of disgrace from him."

And that's the beautiful thing: Gorda doesn't need to hide anything from Friedericke. She, too, is always sickly and tired, sometimes it's her stomach, sometimes her throat hurts, and then she dislocates her shoulder while cleaning the room. What does it matter that I want to sleep in the afternoon if Friedericke also wants to sleep? What does it matter that I want to go to bed early if Friedericke also goes to bed early and wakes up late the next morning? Around Friedericke, I'm entirely normal and reasonable and together and honest when I tell her about my addiction to sleep. "What do you mean by addiction to sleep?" Friedericke says. "You're just tired, as is right and proper." But around Remo I'm tired in a way that is not right and proper.

When Remo comes to me, he wraps himself around me like a blanket, leather outside, fur inside, that is cozy, warm, and surprisingly heavy and that actually weighs down on me like a huge load of blankets, several yards high. And I'm there, at the very bottom, like the tiny pea in the fairy tale and simultaneously, on top, as the princess covered in scratches, which means whining all the time: Oh God, my head hurts so, and just look at those bruises all over my leg. So Remo protects me and presses me and wraps himself around me, and I don't dare move because I might disturb him in his endeavor. But suddenly he remembers me and says: "You won't believe what a comfort it is to be with you completely." So then he isn't the protection, but rather I am. And for that purpose, it's worthwhile to keep completely still and not mention my pounding head and stomach and heart.

I can tell Friedericke about that later.

"Look at my necklace," Gorda says to Friedericke. Friedericke holds it in her hand for a long while and admires the peculiar way the golden links intertwine. "Of course, I had hoped he'd give me a ring for Christmas, but a necklace is nice, too. I can even wear it as a bracelet. Look here. And so I'll always have it with me. Because I'm already wearing my grandmother's locket around my neck, and it doesn't go with the necklace."

"And not one word about getting engaged?"

"Of course not, Friedericke. What are you thinking? My parents know what's proper. We don't live in the nineteenth century anymore."

"Just a touch of the nineteenth century wouldn't hurt."

"What do you mean by that, Friedericke?"

"Well, you know that too: back then your parents would really protect you."

"These days, you just have to protect yourself," Gorda says, strangely upset.

"So, when are you going to Bunten again?" Friedericke asks because she'll be alone then.

"In just three weeks, can you imagine that? He said I should definitely attend his fraternity's annual ball. The dress is a Christmas gift from my parents."

"Oh, that is beautiful," Friedericke says. "Do you mind if I try it on?" Gorda notices with surprise that Friedericke lost a lot of weight during the calorie-rich Christmas weeks. She looks outright emaciated in Gorda's black-pink dress.

"Now if you just changed your hair …" Gorda says and, embarrassed, stops in mid-sentence. I mean what would I say if Friedericke thought my hair too dark. Maybe, she has an issue with her hormones, after all.

In silence, Mother Luck pokes at the pasta casserole with her fork. In silence, she turns her wine glass. And, all of a sudden, she says in standard German—Gorda is so astonished that she's startled—she says in standard German: "That's not fair."

"What's not fair?" Remo asks, also in standard German because he probably knows that what his mother is saying isn't meant for him but for Gorda.

"It's not fair that I pay for your college and don't get to go to the ball."

Remo giggles as if it were a giggling matter.

"It's not fair," Mother Luck repeats one more time. And Gorda quickly gets up to take her shame with herself into the kitchen.

As she put on the black-pink dress, she thinks that the top part is pink because I'm young, and the bottom part is black because I can't enjoy it at all. Mother Luck stands at the door with a look: It's not fair—although she says: "Have fun, you two." But she really means it only for her son. For Gorda she means: The person who pays gets to go to the ball.

And here I go, without having paid the bill, at Remo's side to the ball. And sit with Remo at a table drinking a glass of wine that Remo's mother paid for and that she would like to drink herself. And she would look around with pride: This is my dear son. I, however, look around with sadness: Nothing here is mine. At a table over there is a bride, as if she came to this ball directly from church, in a white sateen dress that has been embroidered with glass beads in order to make her not look like a bride, but she is a bride and remains one with her straight black Snow-White-like hair above her pale shoulders. "They had to marry," Remo giggles, and Gorda wishes they also had to marry but only because Remo cannot live without her. Yet he lives quite comfortably with his mother, who pays all his bills.

Remo's friend Volker is in attendance with a girl who wears a ring on her finger, the most beautiful magic ring that Gorda has seen so far, while Gorda wears one with a small diamond that her father gave her for Christmas, probably because he sensed something about a necklace and no ring—the slender golden type of ring without a stone, the ring that's not really a ring but a protective band. Without it, Christmas remained just Christmas and Gorda was a friend instead of a bride. Volker, however, presents Hanne with the sentence: "Allow me to introduce my bride."

"This is Gorda," Remo says curtly as if he wanted to change the topic. Hanne is from Germany, but she has been working in Switzerland for several years. "Good old Hanne is the accountant in a sausage factory," Remo giggled as though it were a giggling matter; after all, Hanne carries her head nobly, not hunched over like an accountant. The heavy-footed local peasant sounds come forth masterfully from Hanne's mouth. Gorda envies the Renaissance look of Hanne's face in profile, in addition to her middle-high German language skills. She promises herself: In three years, I will just as masterfully speak this almost vanished German. But where is it supposed to come from if Gorda is here so infrequently and if Remo speaks completely modern German?

"You've got to speak Swiss German together," Hanne says as if she guessed Gorda's worries. But Remo glances at her with this look that says the main thing is that I love you—and what are ring and language in comparison to Remo's love?

Gorda has barely opened to door to the room with blue flower design, when Mother Luck's voice rings out. "Help me! Help Me!" she shouts. Well, no, "Reemoo! Reemoo!" But with the intonation of Help me! Help me! So Remo is unsettled and lets go of Gorda's arm, and he runs to the rooms at the back of the apartment. The door closes with a bang behind mother and son. All right then, I've lost him now, Gorda thinks. She rips the unlucky black-pink dress from her body, wipes off the festive and holiday color from her eyes and her cheeks, stares in disgust at her sickly wintry skin in the mirror—why do I always look like I'm suffering from the flu and stomach problems— and carefully opens the door onto the long and dark hallway from the end of which Remo's voice emerges. She hears "music" and "Volker" and "beautiful" and intermittently Mother Luck's middle-high German murmurs, though understandable for Gorda's ear today. "It's not fair," murmurs Mother Luck, and finally the force of trumpets resound through the apartment: "It's not fair!" But Gorda is asleep by then.

"It's going to be your birthday soon," Remo says. "You may wish for whatever you want." And Gorda's wish is for the ring. But an inward wish, please; there are no wishes here that are expressed outwardly.

"Let's go downtown," Gorda says. She spends a long time looking at silver pendants and plain gold loops, but

Remo and Gorda

Remo doesn't think of a ring on his own. And such a ring is no simple ring but a protective band. It can't just be your wish for your birthday. First it has to be Remo's wish for Gorda. And his wish doesn't appear to be anything else but to give her something for her birthday, something quite normal and without symbolic significance, such as a dress, a purse, or shoes.

"Didn't you need boots?" Remo asks.

"Well, yes," and Gorda takes a pair of Bally boots, very nice brown ones with lamb fur around the ankles.

"That's not fair," murmur Mother Luck's silent lips when she sees the boots on Gorda's feet. Just imagine if she were to see a protective band on my left ring finger, that's unimaginable. And, for half an hour, Gorda is almost happy to have gotten the boots for her birthday.

<hr>

Agitated, Remo comes from Mother Luck's room, anxiously closes the door to the room with the blue flower design and isn't really Remo but his mother's son. "Just imagine my brother called and asked my mother if she

already knew that we had gotten engaged. Tell me, do you tell everyone that we've gotten engaged?"

"Of course not."

"And why does somebody called Karin Haller think so?"

"How would I know that?"

"Are you absolutely certain?"

"Of course, I'm certain."

"Can you swear an oath on it?"

Gorda hates swearing an oath. "What kind of awful thing happened that I have to swear an oath on it?"

"By chance, Karin Haller sat at the same table as Jean and Betty during a university function. And then this person, this good old Karin, told Betty that the two of us were engaged. Now my mother is livid, of course. I mean she pays for college, and so she has a right to know if I get engaged." And so she has a right to decide if I get engaged—that's what he means, Gorda thinks. And Remo has no rights, and I have no rights. And the only thing that matters is Remo's love. "Can you swear an oath on that?" And he keeps asking her: "Can you swear an oath on that?"

Gorda swears an oath over and over that she never and in no way as much at even hinted at something so abhorrent as an engagement. Flushed with shame—but only inwardly, nothing is to be seen outwardly here—she remembers her friendly and comforting conversations with Karin Haller, how she had shown her the signet ring, how she had told her about the trip to the Black Forest, about her parents and Remo being on a first-name basis, and about Dad, who paid for everything. And whoever pays is right. But Dad and Mom have no right to demand: "Young man, explain yourself." That sort of right belongs in the last century. In this century, all rights are on the side of the young man. And he says: "Swear an oath that you've never claimed that we're engaged. And the only thing that matters is our love."

At that moment, Gorda knows that love doesn't count for anything, and that the only thing that counts in his life is who pays his bills.

To pay for Remo's work and leisure hours, Mother Luck has made great sacrifices. A civil servant's pension isn't that much, don't have any illusions about that. So she partitioned the entire house into apartments, each room with a kitchenette and a bath. They are tiny student apartments, except that she doesn't rent to students, of whom Bunten does have some, but to guest workers from Italy. And they make quite a racket. There are four families upstairs and four families with children downstairs and a new child every year. You can imagine the shrieks and laughs and whining and shouts throughout the house. On the first of each month, Mother Luck sits behind her desk in the living room and receives the heads of the guest worker families from Italy, the most beautiful country in the world, like a Swiss queen, but she really was just a German by birth. And she has them give her rent for the rooms that are as expensive as apartments. Everywhere in Switzerland these sorts of rooms are just as expensive for Italians, there's nothing unusual about it. And she also sells them the laundry detergent for the washing machines that she had kindly set up in the basement. This makes it easier for the guests to stay in Switzerland, and Mother Luck can be certain that no second-rate Italian detergent will destroy the good Swiss machines. And one hot summer evening, she even started selling fresh, cool beer. It was incredibly practical for the people to have everything in one house under one roof. But the inn next door didn't go along with that because Mother Luck didn't have a license for that, and so she almost got sued. Thus, she has made many sacrifices to pay for Remo's university studies in Germany and in Switzerland and has paid for the right over Remo's engagement.

"When he kept repeating swear-an-oath-swear-an-oath, something inside me broke, Friedericke. You understand that, don't you?"

Friedericke understands and holds Gorda's hand, the hand with the small diamond ring, which reminds her daily of the other ring, the slender golden one that is a protective band. And a dagger in Mother Luck's chest.

When Remo came to her on the last evening, he no longer was an enveloping blanket, leather outside and fur inside, but just ballast, many yards high, and the princess underneath with an aching stomach, pounding heart, and a rat in her head.

"There's always something wrong with you," the prince says angrily and slams the door behind him.

———

Friedericke's head now radiates with fully blonde hair where there used to be sad ash sprinkled in. And her glasses are in their case because suddenly Friedericke is able to see without them or maybe not, but you usually don't notice. Only when, for example, she tries to place the cake plate on top of the candle holder or the fork next to the vase instead of Botho's cherry tart. Moved, he looks at her as if for a last time; and, moved, Gorda looks a Botho and Friedericke as if for a last time. And Friedericke laughs her new laugh that she got for Christmas; she has never laughed like that before. Gorda feels her mouth sagging. No tart will help in this case, at best, maybe, a glass of wine. And Gorda has three, for starters.

On Tuesday, Gorda gets a letter from Dad. But Dad never writes, and now there are five pages in painstakingly drawn calligraphy. My dear daughter, he writes, and he's never called her my dear daughter. She is just his stepdaughter and sometimes not even that when Dad is in a bad mood and says to Mom: "Tell your daughter she should cut her coat according to her cloth." My dear daughter, and Gorda doesn't believe her own eyes: I would like to let you know that you have inherited a rather substantial amount of money from your grandmother … I've worked hard to preserve and increase it over all these years … you do not come from the most modest background … and have every reason to hold your head high … no need to feel ashamed and hide from anyone—especially not from any of the families there—never mind the professor-brother nor the dissertation on Conrad Ferdinand Meyer. And so it went on page after page from this taciturn man: anger sharpened his pen, and pride made him spread his wings.

"Just listen to this," Gorda says to Friedericke. "My mother must have told him about this swear-an-oath-swear-an-oath; otherwise, I can't explain his writing frenzy. Actually, he wrote the letter for Remo and Mother Luck and not for me. Now, should I let them read it or not?"

Friedericke had left Thursday to visit her aunt, and Gorda writes a letter to Remo. Do I tell him about the letter or not? At that moment, the doorbell rings, and in walks Botho with a bottle of wine. "What a coincidence," Gorda says. "I wasn't sure whether I really was in the mood for writing." She lights a candle and drinks a glass of wine, which brings light to her heart. There's a dire need of light in her heart. Botho talks about the seminary he must absolutely join next semester, which means good-bye to the nice drives to the blue-tinged forests, good-bye wine and cherry tarts, the meat fondues, and the midnight chicken legs with Friedericke and Gorda.

"But you have to eat something," Gorda asks terrified. "Or do future priests live on thin air?"

"We live on God's love," Botho says as though he were speaking of something horrible. And Gorda hears Remo's voice: "The only thing that matters is our love."

"At least, God's love is not dependent on any mother," Gorda says.

Surprised, Botho asks: "What kind of mother are you talking about?"

"Remo's mother, of course." And then she tells him about it's-not-fair and swear-an-oath-swear-an-oath (by that time, they've started on the second bottle) and about Dad's letter and the practical Bally shoes although she spent half an hour, so it seemed to her, standing in front of the display with the thirty or so protective bands. "In the end, I get a pair of boots. Just imagine that. That's just like a slap in the face." And she goes to get the boots. "Here, they're yours for the seminary." And Gorda and Botho laugh as if they shed an unfathomable burden, the burden of God's love and the burden of Remo's love. And as Botho takes her into his arms, she knows nothing of a blanket, leather outside and fur inside, and under it the scratched-up princess with aching stomach and pounding heart and a rat in her brain.

She's perfectly healthy.

Friedericke can't possibly already know of their midnight transgression, and yet she looks at them as if she were suffering from an aching stomach. "I feel funny today," she tells Botho as he is about to eat his daily piece of cherry tart. "I think I should go to bed." He sets the bottle of wine down onto the table like someone who has to apologize and knows he's not going to. And he leaves. And Gorda also goes to bed like someone who has some explaining to do but can't explain it and, therefore, prefers to read in bed. So, over the next few days, she's always reading whenever Friedericke looks over to her.

"Tell me, what are you reading so intently?" Friedericke asks finally.

"Goethe's *Elective Affinities*," Gorda says as if that would explain anything.

Goethe, etching from *Elective Affinities*

149

"Do you know this newspaper article," Gorda asks Remo on her next visit.

"Where did you get that from?" Remo says in a tone that means: That's none of your business.

"I found it in the book over there," Gorda says although it had been in the back of the drawer in Remo's desk. Remo takes the article like a piece of soiled laundry and reads.

"Oh, well," he says as if it left him speechless.

"Professor Gordon is in prison?" Gorda asks, agitated.

"He's in detention pending trial, not in prison," Remo corrects her.

"And why is he in detention pending trial?"

"He made a risky investment."

"What kind of risky investment?"

"Well, he bought a piece of land in Australia on the assumption it would increase in value. And he sold shares on it. Too many shares. He just made a mistake."

"And you go to prison for that?"

"He's in pretrial detention, I already told you that."

"It says here: picked up by police, three police cars even, and taken away in handcuffs. That sounds more like a dangerous criminal. The press pounced all over this case like a starving lion on a gerbil. Why didn't you tell me anything about it?"

"Jean didn't want me to talk about it."

"And you just do what your brother tells you to?"

"Just stop already," Remo says tersely. "Why are you even concerned with my brother's friend."

"Why am I even concerned with his brother's friend, he said, Friedericke. As though his brother's friend weren't the father of the girl that Remo was supposed to marry. That Remo, maybe, is still supposed to marry. But now she won't be getting millions as her father had wanted. And as Remo's brother had wanted when he wanted Justi for Remo."

When Gorda thinks of the apartment in Bunten, then she thinks of the letters in the book covers, the letters in drawers and cupboards, the letters in dresser and small boxes under the bed. "That apartment is stuffed full with books and letters, Friedericke. All you need to do is to open anything, let's say a dictionary, and a letter comes tumbling toward you. For decades, they've kept their entire correspondences as though they had a book about their family in mind, a kind of family saga, that someone would write about them sometime. So, one day, this biographer would show up and say: 'May I have a look at your letters?' Because such old documents are of unimaginable value. Or they all believe they all are born writers or, at least, letter writers. I've never seen so many letters brought to life."

"Well, do you read their letters?" Friedericke asks surprised.

"You know, I read one here or there. You'd do the same if you felt an enemy lurking in every book, under every bed, in every dresser, in all the drawers. And, of course, you want to know who your enemy is."

Whenever Remo wasn't there, Gorda read the letters, her room with the blue flower design is full of them, after all. The longest ones are from Jean, who gives guidance to his fatherless younger brother like a father: I didn't become a writer, but one day you certainly will, it says in one of those fatherly letters of guidance. Jean wants to encourage Remo with that guidance. You're everything that I was supposed to be, he means to say. But isn't he saying at the same time: You must be everything that I wanted to be; otherwise, you're nothing? And, perhaps for this reason, Remo is rewriting the beginning of his dissertation on Conrad Ferdinand Meyer for the twelfth time now—because he's writing it as a writer, not a professor? For him, there's no adjective catchy enough, no noun flexible enough, no sentence structure matching his tremendous expectations of scholarly flow and fine, plainly beautiful power of expression. Jean edited the fifty pages, Betty studied the fifty pages, Gorda took them apart with care, put them back together again, and thought: If he continues at this pace, we still won't be engaged in ten years. Because without his dissertation, there's no engagement. That's a fact as firm as the Child Eater Fountain at Bunten's Market Square. Jean had mentioned linguistic weaknesses, and now Remo is studying linguistic strengths instead of continuing to study the works of Conrad Ferdinand Meyer. Currently, he hasn't been writing a dissertation on Conrad Ferdinand Meyer but a language exercise on the topic of "author or scholar, that is the question." As if Mother Luck had said to Jean: Prevent him from getting engaged to this person. And now Jean's criticism prevents Remo from finishing his dissertation. Nevertheless, he continues to ask: "Remo, how's your dissertation coming?" Gorda believes she should help and intervene. But when she said to Remo: "I don't think you should show Jean your dissertation anymore," he yelled: "Stay out of my family affairs!" And when she said: "This picture is crooked," he yelled: "What do you know about how to hang pictures!" But later he straightened out the picture. She took note of that.

In secret, she counts the pages of his dissertation in Bunten: fifty three, fifty four, fifty five, fifty six, six pages in five weeks. That's about one page per week. "How many pages do these dissertations typically have?" She asked Remo as inconspicuously as possible. "Well, roughly 250 to 500 pages although some go up to 800 pages." Gorda turns pale but, please, inwardly please, nothing is shown outwardly here. Then it'll take ten years, and we still won't be engaged!

When Friedericke is visiting her aunt again, Botho comes over to Gorda without a bottle of wine. "Hey, let's take a ride around the area here. I know of a nice restaurant."

While they eat, he talks about the seminary, where he will eat again from tin cups like he used to during his childhood.

"And then I can forget all of this," he says and points from the delicious goulash dish with spaetzle and roasted green beans and carrots to the decanter with red wine.

Gorda tells about the labors of a dissertation that obviously doesn't want to be birthed. "You know, it's been stalled on page sixty-four for three months. He just keeps revising instead of adding on to it."

"Why are you concerned about his dissertation?" Botho asks sullenly.

"I'm concerned about it a whole lot: it's the green light to my protective band. As long as he hasn't finished, I see a red light."

At home, Botho pulls her on the bed.

"Botho, stop it," Gorda says, but then she doesn't stop herself. "And what's to become of us?"

"I won't enter the seminary, then," Botho says, "and you don't go to Bunten to a mother-in-law who hates you."

"Yes, yes," Gorda says while she kisses him. And then says: "No, no, certainly not. The only thing that matters is Remo's love."

Two days later, Gorda gets a call from the hospital. Botho ran his car into a parked truck while on the way to his furnished room. He probably had been thinking about the seminary and had been looking toward his future in desperation instead of looking at the present. "Come here immediately," says the nurse. So Friedericke and Gorda go to Botho with flowers and wine and cherry tart, and they shed tears on his neck. Yet he sheds no tears at all: "A priest with a cane, that's out of the question, of course," he explains. "I'll pursue an academic career as professor, English or history. I still need to decide." And he already looks as though he were carrying his head full of books.

"I talked it over with my aunt," Friedericke says. "She wants to support me when it comes to my father. She'll come to Leerheide, and I don't have to do anything. My aunt is quite a fighter, I tell you. And when she leaves for home, then I'll already be enrolled in veterinary school in Münster."

"And I'll take up the studies of the secrets of beautiful sentences in Switzerland again," Gorda says defiantly. Let her parents say you've-got-to-see-it-through-to-the-bitter-end. I'll determine the bitter end myself.

———

"No," Mom says in a loud voice, "you just can't change you major again. That won't work at all."

"But I'm just changing back," Gorda says. "What's so terrible about it? It must be possible to change one's mind?"

"You keep changing your mind all the time! Dad said, you're done changing you major."

"Can't you talk with him again about it?"

"No, I won't do that under any circumstances!" Mom yells as though she were fed up with the argument. And Gorda thinks: My own mother exiles me to everlasting unhappiness.

———

At night, she dreams of a huge diamond diadem that floats next to Mom in the ocean, but when it starts sinking, Mom doesn't reach for it. So Gorda dives after it, wild with fear.

I've got to dive for my happiness in the same way, she thinks the next morning. She puts on her wetsuit and approaches Dad with the words: "I want to take up the studies of the secrets of beautiful sentences in Switzerland."

He just laughs: "Well, that makes me just laugh!"

"Then I'll look for a job there."

"Look for a job there," Dad repeats in an icy look.

"First, I'll take a couple of French courses, then I'll look for a job there," Gorda tells Remo on the phone.

"So you want to drop out of university?" He asks in surprise.

No, no, Gorda thinks (but inwardly, please, nothing is shown outwardly here) and says: "Yes, yes."

"The only thing that matters is our love," she hears Remo say as she is about to hang up. The only thing that matters are my studies, Gorda thinks. The diadem can't be allowed to sink and disappear.

My aunt dueled with my father for three days, Friedericke writes, because he didn't even know that I had already enrolled in veterinary school. So there was nothing to duel about. And Botho doesn't have to use the cane for the rest of his life, either. He's already breezing light-footed through Freiburg's History department and eats cherry tart at Meyer's bakery, on his way, and, in the evening, goulash or veal cutlets in the little restaurant next to our vegetable shop, you know where that is. So there's nothing of tin cup or oversalted food in God's love.

The only thing that matters are our studies, Gorda writes.

She took the sleeper car overnight to Basel, then there was the train ride with sunshine all the way to Lausanne: there are vineyards left and right and below is Lake Geneva with mountains to the left and plains to the right. Or are those just clouds? Above her head lie her possessions: the marshland prints that induce the feeling of home, the black-brown wool blanket that invites you to relax (wherever it is, that is your home), and her skirts and blouses and sweaters to cover her anxieties. Oh, my God, what kind of mousy heart beats in this sweater? This will be the third city in two years, the third start, the third end. Cornelia, what are you doing this evening? Marion, I've always liked you. Karin, I forgive you for gossiping about my engagement. Friedericke, my dearest friend, do write often.

———

She takes a cab to the hotel for which she had made reservations from Oldenburg. It's small and run-down on the outside, but the room has a view, no, a kind of hatch that opens toward the lake. Gorda spends an hour letting her gaze slip into the lake as if she could fish for courage. Instead of going to the university, she first goes to bed. Home—the bed sheets whisper. Home—the pillows sob. Home—the down comforter shrieks. With all the noise, Gorda can't possibly sleep. So she takes one of Botho's pills that emanate calmness.

When she wakes up, it's too late to go to campus. So she'll look for a room tomorrow. Today offers the sandwiches Mom made and the book about Goethe's arrival in Weimar. He had the heart of a leopard. The little mouse in Gorda's chest, however, doesn't want to set one foot out the door. No one can get me out of this room. Tomorrow, you've got to leave whether you want to or not. A gorge, a red maw, a giant crater of a gorge opens up before her and, screaming, she tumbles into it. And, screaming, she keeps plunging. And, screaming, she lands with a smack on the hardwood floor. Goethe never screamed for his mother like this.

The next morning, her eyes bulge out as if they were still screaming for something. Sunglasses help; otherwise, everyone would see what condition she was in. At the student housing office, there is a young man with an Italian face and a French tongue. "You seem to feel a little lonely," he says in German when he notices that Gorda doesn't understand him. Just gives a quick nod because she's afraid of bursting into tears. "I know some very nice people for you: Here, that's the address of my parents."

Gorda takes a cab, and ten minutes later she rings the doorbell at Mrs. Pache's. "Poor child," she says in French and shows Gorda to her room because, certainly, she won't keep looking for a room if she already has one. Her new home must have once belonged to the son in the student housing office when he still was going to high school. It has the necessary desk at the window, a bed, and a rocking chair with a lamp if you like to sit and read, which Gorda doesn't want to do because she prefers reading in bed.

Just a few hours later—after she had retrieved her suitcase from the hotel and unpacked it—Gorda is sitting at her desk (as though it had always been her desk) and writes to Remo, who is doing his annual military service in the Swiss Jura region. Madame Pache has three parrots, two green ones and one gray, all of whom can yodel. Just imagine three yodeling parrots in the kitchen! Of course, I've got to laugh when I hear them, and I hear them all day long because the kitchen is but three steps away from my room. But what she doesn't write is this: If I laugh, I'm at least not able to scream out in fear.

On Sunday, Remo travels from the Jura region to spend a couple of hours in Lausanne. Gorda meets him at the train station. He is wearing his gray uniform and Gorda thinks of war, but only for a brief moment because he pushes the both of them into a passport photo booth. The photo strip shows two grinning faces without war and without fear. Oh, how beautiful the world is! We're young and together, and what

does it matter that Remo didn't dare tell his mother that he's visiting me and not her. "I just said that I had to stay in the Jura region." They take the subway to the lake. Remo knows his way around in this city. And for the first time, Gorda walks with Remo along the banks of the oblong-shaped lake, to the left are the Alps; to the right, the plains; above us the cherry trees in full bloom; and tulips at our feet. What does it matter that, just a few days before, you were screaming and tossing and turning on the hardwood floor in a little run-down hotel?

To get to the École de Français Moderne, Gorda has to take the streetcar to a modern-practical square where all streetcars originate and terminate. Then she walks up the stairs and steps through a gate into Lausanne's old town: no more concrete and gray and dreary tracks for the streetcars. Here there are green window shutters next to flower boxes with bundles of manicured red geraniums, giant chestnut trees, and wide palace-like buildings where the École is located. Further back, the brightly scrubbed medieval cathedral shines from the top of the city hill. It looks cozy: like a small town just for university studies inside the city. In the modern part, people live and shop, cook and honk; here we read and understand, research, rethink. Here you don't get any other ideas except those that you should have for your studies. Even the Café Soleil offers a direct view into the rooms of the library. And if you always have books in your sight, wherever you sit, then reading and learning is much easier.

Gorda registers for many courses in the École de Français Moderne: Grammar, vocabulary, textual studies, pronunciation, literature, translation, and French and Swiss history. You can never take enough classes in case you won't be able to take classes anymore. This is my last chance, Gorda thinks. And she adds another course on François Mauriac. That adds up to twenty-three hours of classes per week. So, there won't be much time left to be afraid.

There is, of course, no sign of amphitheaters in small medieval university towns. So you sit again in small, dark classrooms, a chalkboard in front and, next to it, the teacher who's now called professor, usually not holding a chalkboard pointer in hand but often a piece of chalk. With it, he proves the beauty of the secrets of the French language, which seem to Gorda just as interesting as the secrets of the beautiful German sentences. You eat lunch at the Foyer Restaurant Universitaire, which does sound much more appetizing than student cafeteria, on a tiny hill across from the cathedral. Gorda shared a table with Vreni, who is at the École in Gorda's classes on grammar and textual studies and François Mauriac. "I'm from Oldenburg," Gorda said, in the quiet voice that you use when you know that you say something dumb. Vreni must have also thought she was saying something dumb because her voice was very quiet. But then her voice grew louder, and so did Gorda's. So finally they had a regular conversation— spoken, not whispered. Vreni comes from Linzingen, which is, in contrast to Oldenburg, not far away at all, just a couple of hours by train, so she can go home every weekend. She has it good, Gorda thinks.

Postcard of Lausanne (detail)

"It means that I have to go home every weekend," Vreni says. "Do you think, Miss Gorda, I want to go home all the time? It's much nicer here in Lausanne."

Later, when they drink coffee together in the Soleil, they already have dropped the 'Miss' and use just first names, which is, in Gorda's mind, a promise that Vreni will have coffee with her many more times.

Her grammar class shows that Gorda hasn't studied grammar since high school. Her vocabulary class shows that Gorda hasn't studied vocabulary since high school. Her translation class shows that the other students have French mothers or Swiss mothers who speak French or fathers who speak French or teachers who speak French. Or all of the above. Gorda, however, had German teachers who taught French and a German father and a German mother. So, of course, she can't keep up. She's got to limp along behind everyone else. Nonsense, it's not a matter of limping along; she has to stay on the road of learning. And under no circumstances does she want to fall by the wayside. After all, Dad and Mom don't want her to go to university, and Remo already has said that our love is the only thing that matters, and then the person who pays is the one who counts, and not our love.

How can you overcome French mothers and French fathers, Gorda thinks in desperation. And she goes to the Librairie Payot and buys a book she's always wanted to read: *Memoirs of a Dutiful Daughter*, by Simone de Beauvoir. And she buys it in German as well as in French. At Madame Pache's, she puts the

French book on the left side of her desk and the German book on the right side. And on the left, her index finger reads the French sentence and, on the the right, her index finger reads the German sentence. In this manner, French-on-the-left-German-on-the-right, she reads sentence after sentence almost as quickly as she would read it solely in German. And while she is amazed by Simone de Beauvoir's leopard's heart, she learns French left hand down.

Only now does she fully comprehend the sentence: I accomplished it hands down.

———

"That's why Volker got engaged. He was forced into doing it," Remo said and giggled a lot.

"Stop giggling," Gorda said in the restaurant on Lake Geneva and pushed the lukewarm mineral water away from her. "How can anyone be forced to get engaged?"

"Oh, well, he wasn't really forced, just half-forced." Remo couldn't stop giggling. The lake looked light-blue, and the mountains shimmered in brownish hues with white portions of snow on top, which looked like eternal whipped cream on eternal hazelnut ice cream. A picture to sink your sweet tooth into, Gorda thought, and for a moment, things like forced engagements no longer existed. All you needed to do was to look at this picture, and all engagements were wished for and no longer protective bands but, instead, an open park where you could take strolls heart in heart without fear of annoying Mother-Luck glances. Yet as soon as Remo looked at Gorda, the dream of the open park disappeared, and the forced engagement returned. "Well, just tell me how she forced him."

"She went back to Germany to her hometown of Xanten for a year "and again was the beloved child in her parents' home and not the hated future daughter-in-law in Bunten."

"And now she's well-liked as a bride in Bunten?" Gorda asked. What she would've loved to ask the most: "Maybe I should go back to Oldenburg, too?" But she let it slide. He might have even answered "yes." And if he hadn't, his mother would have, for sure.

———

Vreni speaks with such a cute medieval accent which, however, doesn't impede comprehension. Her eyes look up chocolate-brown from her face, which she keeps lowered all the time as though she were ashamed of something, but Gorda doesn't know of what. Not of her thick, light-brown curls, her classically rounded lips, her skillfully upward-swinging nose. Not of her slender body with her delicate wrists, where she wears gold jewelry, which is really delicate, barely visible, so thin are the bracelets, so narrow is the wristwatch. Gorda would've liked to have such a narrow wristwatch. From Dad or preferably from Remo, if it can't be a protective band.

Since Gorda began studying in Lausanne, Remo's mother has been studying the walls whenever Gorda visits. Is there someone visiting? Her look says. No one visiting me, in any case. Without looking and without a word, she stares at the nightly catastrophes on TV. Even Remo gets hardly a look or word when Gorda is there. Maybe she talks at him incessantly when I'm not there: Whoever moves to my country wants to move into my house, and I decide who moves into my house. "You've got to forgive her," Remo told Gorda. "Just image she isn't here. And the only thing that counts is our love." How can I imagine she's not here when she already imagines I'm not here? No one is more present than the person you imagine is not there. It's as if the two of us were here twice. So from now on, Mother Luck is present twice from now on: once as a person and once as a person being thought away. And the thought-away person even enters the room with the blue flower design, accompanies Gorda into the bathroom, goes downtown with her, and finally goes to bed with her. No one can stand this, Gorda thinks. This imagine-she's-not-here has got to stop as soon as possible.

Falling in love with Lausanne is an easy step for Gorda. She doesn't have to walk along its streets for weeks to generate a feeling of home, she doesn't have to conquer the cafés to feel: I've always come here to drink coffee. No one has to drag her from bed to stroll down Rue de Bourg past hundreds of shops all the way to the square, which looks again like the ecclesiastical Middle Ages; however, the large, bright buildings and their wide façades with windows are clearly most likely nineteenth century. And the lake is visible no matter where you are, because Lausanne climbs up a hill where wine used to grow, like it still does today to the left and to the right and above the city. Lausanne is a business town with a garland of foliage around it, a medieval university town and a place of entertainment on the ocean, well, on the lake, which is as large as a small ocean.

At the beginning of June, the joys of the lake start at the public beaches, where Gorda sits with Vreni in the afternoons as soon as their classes are over. Then Vreni talks about Mathias.

Vreni's parents don't want Mathias in Vreni's life. But Vreni wants Mathias in her life all the more. "I mean, if they gave me time to think about it, I could actually think about it, but they won't give me time."

"Why don't your parents want Mathias in your life?"

"That's complicated." So, Vreni and Mathias went to school together, but Mathias is German, not Swiss. And from northern Germany to boot. Although he can now speak the medieval dialect perfectly. "You can't tell the difference, really," says Vreni.

Gorda thinks if he could learn it, why can't I? "Well, I don't see the problem. Mathias is not just from northern Germany, but he's also the son of an actor and director of the municipal theater in Linzingen," Gorda says.

"Well, his parents are divorced. And we're Catholic, after all. All of Linzingen is Catholic, did you know that?" Gorda didn't know that. "And his father is living with a female dancer, no, with two female dancers, but the second one will move out soon, Mathias said. For Linzingen, one dancer would already be too many, you see. You've got to come visit me, Gorda. I'll introduce you to Mathias.

Since Gorda started studying in Lausanne, Remo and she have been talking a lot on the phone. She walks over to a phone booth at the end of the street where she lives, and waits for his call. And the call's always right on time. You can rely on Remo. Since Gorda started studying in Lausanne, she hasn't wanted to visit Bunten anymore. "Come here," she says every Thursday evening as they discuss their plans for the weekend. "No, you come here this time," Remo says. "My mother is expecting a visitor, so I can't leave." The visitor's name is Wilhelm, who's an old friend of Remo's mother and his father, when he was still alive, and who's a new friend of Remo's mother now as they are both widowed, Wilhelm and beautiful Elsie from the old days. "Wilhelm called us right after his wife's funeral," Remo said, giggling. "And I told my mother: 'Go ahead and just invite him.' You know that would be good for her if she weren't always alone." Why would she be alone, Gorda thinks. She's got her son, after all. And whom do I have?

And now two couples sit in the Bunten apartment: the old one and the young one. Speaking among themselves, the old couple speaks Middle Ages and the young one modern times. This way, you don't notice that the modern times don't understand the Middle Ages and that the Middle Ages don't want to understand the modern times. Remo's real mother is busy, the only one still in the way is the one who's being imagined away. She keeps saying: "I decide who comes into my house." As soon as Wilhelm has left, Mother Luck calls out again from her rooms at the back: "Help me! Help me!"—no, "Reemoo! Reemoo!" But it sounds like "Help me! Help me!" and, distressed, Remo hurries to the rooms in the back, and Gorda thinks: Well, I've lost him now. I've not only lost him for now, I've never had him. His mother has a firm hold on him inside her walls. All she needs to do is to call "Reemoo! Reemoo," and I'm completely alone in the world, here in the room with the blue flower design. Well, being completely alone would still be nice, but I'm here alone with the mother I imagine away, who imagines me away, too, and can't get rid of me because the more she imagines me away, the stronger

I come back. This has to stop, this thing with thinking each other away. I can't take it anymore.

But Gorda takes it because she's got a home now in Lausanne with a father, a mother, and three children. These are Monsieur and Madame Pache and the three parrots, two green and a gray one. The gray one wants to be green and plucks out his gray feathers so that green ones may grow. But the green ones don't want to come in. Likewise, I keep plucking the gray feathers so that I won't be the unloved girlfriend in Bunten but the well-liked bride. But the green feathers don't want to come in. At Monsieur and Madame Pache's, however, Gorda is already entirely green-feathered, that's how well-liked she is there. In the evenings, Madame Pache calls "Goda! Goda!" which sounds like "Coco! Coco!" which is the prettier of the green parrots. And in the narrow kitchen, Gorda eats dinner, or *dîner* as it's called here, with Monsieur and Madame. And when Monsieur Pache says, *à votre santé*, then the table wine tastes better than any conceited and noble wine in the big gloomy dining room in Bunten. After the meal, Monsieur Pache lets the parrots come out of their cages, and as we drink coffee and eat cookies, gray-green feathers flutter about our cups. The parrots begin to yodel "because they like to yodel only when free," Monsieur Pache says. "In the cage, they are too sad to sing." Actually, they don't yodel, they rejoice for the glory of God like highly talented nightingales. This is how Gorda would like to rejoice in Bunten one day.

Monsieur and Madame Pache not only share roasts and soups with Gorda, they also share their French with her. Every day, she gets one morsel more on her way to the university.

Yesterday, it was "J'ai mal au dos," and today it is "Je souffre plus que hier" because Madame Pache has back pain, in her *dos*, and is barely able to clean house. Monsieur Pache does that for her. And when she says that she isn't feeling well today: "Je suis pas bien aujourd'hui," then she laughs as though she were saying that today is the most beautiful day in her life. It seems as though you'd bear pain more gracefully in French than in German.

Lizzy is visiting in Bunten, Lizzy without her parents because Betty is expecting their second child, but Lizzy doesn't believe that. "They don't want me anymore," she whispered to Gorda. "They won't ever come to pick me up." As she told Gorda, she hugged and squeezed Gorda: "Mama, Mama, don't leave me alone." Gorda hugged the child as though that made her hers, hers and Remo's. Lizzy looks indeed like Remo with her thick black hair and her gray eyes, and she could be hers, too.

This was exactly what angered Remo: "Just let the child be," he snapped with his beamlike eyebrows pulled tightly together as if the child didn't need her but she needed the child. Which was true, in fact. Now more than ever, Gorda thought. And no sooner thought than done, Gorda held Lizzy in her arms whenever she wanted to be held. "I told you to stop fussing about the child," Remo snapped again, and his lips formed a sharp line. He's jealous of a child, so will he one day be jealous of his own child? That would be horrible. Oh, you poor child of ours, better stay in children's heaven.

As she returns to the living room, Lizzy leans over Remo's bare feet, which he's pulled up on a chair. "Now I know why you love him," she says in English as if she'd solved an unsolvable mystery, "because of the smell of his feet." But with the exception of his feet, she can't stand him. "Don't go! Don't go!" she yelled when Gorda left, who would've preferred to stay to be a protective band around little Lizzy. Whenever you are such a protective band, you forget for a while that you yourself need the same kind of protective band.

Gorda has a new girl friend whose name is Eva, as is her nature, but not at all like the Eve from Paradise with lowered head and somehow ashamed; rather, she holds her head high and looks around: Where are the pretty girls in this land? And the pretty girls of the land look back at Eva's childlike head with its little childlike nose and chubby cheeks and dimples when she laughs like a child. Men like pretty children when they aren't children anymore. Eva is already twenty-one and still a virgin. "That's got to come to an end," she told Gorda. "It's an outright shame." To bring this outright shame to an honorable end, Eva always sits off to the side at the public beach, which means not with Gorda and Vreni and the other female students of the École. "There's no boy who will approach such a bunch of girls," Eva told Gorda as they were walking to class. From now on, she also intends on walking to the École by herself. Who knows, maybe the right one shows up and you just block him from seeing me, well, that can't be, you do understand?"

So Eva is always ready to meet the right guy, but that guy has to always lie in bed at home or sit in the wrong café or know a different public beach, or he's on a sailboat out on the lake this very moment. The wrong guys, however, keep on approaching Eva in the École, they run after her all the way to her furnished room, they phone her from some obscure pub, they forward her letters from some unknown guy who claims to have seen her in this or that restaurant, above all the Mövenpick, which everyone here calls Möpi, and who's wrestled her address from a mutual female acquaintance. Eva's child-like face always attracts the wrong guys. The right guys must love grown-up noses and grown-up chins and grown-up lips and cheeks. Yet no human being is as grown up as Eva.

This Friday, Gorda didn't go to Bunten but to Linzingen with Vreni. Her parents are away on a trip, so it's a good time. "Do you even know where you're going?" Rosemarie, who's also from Linzingen, asked Gorda.

"No, why?"

"You're going to one of the wealthiest families in Linzingen: the concrete plant Kantig, the architect's office

View of Linzingen's main street

Kantig, structural and civil engineering Kantig, the chocolate factory Kantig."

That can't be true! My little Vreni with her head down, her dear hangdog look, and delicate gold jewelry? Wouldn't she at least be wearing bangles as thick as thumbs?

But it turns out to be true. Vreni lives in a mansion built on a slope in the city with full view of famous Lake Linzingen and an unobstructed view of towering mountains to the left and to the right and in the middle. Below is a precious carved wooden bridge from the fourteenth century and in the garden, which is in the middle of the city and yet a large garden, there's a swimming pool so blue as though you were looking at a mountain lake. Vreni doesn't have to do any cooking either because the mansion is like a well-run hotel, a private hotel with a private cook and a private chauffeur and a private gardener and a private maid.

"Here, these are my rooms," Vreni says. "Just look at all these things that my mother bought so that I'll forget Mathias and, like clothes, put on Stefan or Georg or any of the boys of the leading Catholic families in Linzingen: medical products, china factory, clock production, banks. Vreni pulls open the doors to the built-in closets and angrily points to the piles of cashmere sweaters, silk blouses, linen dresses, Hermes scarves. To the hangers of carefully lined up skirts, pants, jackets, and overcoats by world-renowned manufacturers. "The evening dresses here—I'm supposed to wear them to parties, these awful dances meant to marry off rich folk. But without me," Vreni says. "This means nothing to me." It might have meant something to Gorda. Hasn't she always yearned for green feathers? Here's a girl decked out in nothing but green, and she tears out her feathers and would like to be gray.

If Gorda came from such a mansion in Linzingen, Mother Luck would be lucky to receive such a daughter-in-law as a guest in her gloomy, half-rustic and half-aristocratic living room.

Vreni's parents, in contrast, don't want to receive in their mansion a son-in-law who comes from a Protestant household that overflows with female dancers. That's why they handed over a picture postcard—one of the kind that says "Many greetings from Oberammergau"—to a handwriting expert who confirmed the parents' wish to hear that Mathias was a gold digger interested only in the family's huge architectural firm and not really in Vreni, who'd just be some kind of worthless decoration in the gift basket. Mathias does plan on being an architect. "I'm sure my parents paid that expert a royal sum for that expert opinion," Vreni says scornfully. You wouldn't have expected so much scorn in such a delicate and humble person. "Mathias didn't even write in his normal cursive handwriting but in capital letters so that I'd be able to read everything easily. He tends to scrawl, you know. But the expert said all of this would be proof of his underlying tendency to being a fraud and confidence man, to desiring chocolate and being addicted to concrete. That's just laughable." And Vreni laughs the laugh that you laugh without laughing.

That afternoon, they meet Mathias at the lake and sit in a Linzingen café with a view of the famous covered bridge. He looks like he comes from up there on the map, where black-haired Gorda comes from and all the boys with reddish-blond hair and with blue eyes and pale eye lashes and a skin without sunshine, that is, perfectly normal in Gorda's eyes. And he speaks perfect modern German, as well as medieval German, without accent—the modern version with swift eloquence and the old with easy-going slowness. Back then people took horse and carriage throughout their lives; today they take the race car. That has to show in language somehow. And Mathias is here now and gone the next moment and still here but always on the go. No wonder that Vreni loves him. In him, she loves the past and the future simultaneously, which is always the most beautiful kind of love. Now Gorda also understands what Vreni is ashamed of: the rank growth of her parents' wealth, just as Mathias is ashamed of his father's female dancers or, at least, of the one who's too many. And, in Bunten, Gorda is ashamed of her gray feathers. Yet as the three of them are laughing over a cup of coffee, they aren't ashamed of anything.

———

When Gorda visits Bunten again, Jean had already picked up Lizzy to finally show her new little brother to her. The following afternoon, Mother Luck went to Wilhelm, and Remo accompanied her. Gorda stayed in bed as if the rat were in her head although it just was in her heart. With a quick movement and without thinking, she reached with her hand under the bed, fished around, and felt an unknown box, strained to pull it out and emptied it onto the bed. Oh, all those letters from Jean! What a born letter writer he is and what a born surrogate father for his little brother.

"My dear Remo," he addresses him. Gorda twitches every time she reads the word "my." My dear Remo, I don't want to

174

interfere in your affairs—and then he proceeds to interfere in his affairs. Gorda knows that she should stop, but then she takes the next letter: My dear Remo, I know you're now old enough to know what you're doing—and then he tells him what to do. Gorda knows her name will show up soon. And then her name does show up, and there'd still be time to put down the letter with all the others and put the box back under the bed. But she can't. I've got to know who my enemy is. You're making a big mistake, believe me, Jean writes. In contrast, Justi has the right manner, and you said yourself that she was particularly nice when you met her at Wilhelm's place …

Remo met with Justi at Wilhelm's place! And where is he today? At Wilhelm's place! Didn't he seem quite relieved when I pretended to have a headache and said: "Better go by yourself." Remo meets with Justi at Wilhelm's or downtown while I lie in bed with the rat, even though it isn't in my head but my heart. And if no terrible punishment is doled out just now, I'll have the rat in my head, too. Just you wait, I'll make you pay for this. And Gorda goes to Remo's room, opens the little wall cabinet above his dresser, and empties it of the letters inside—they are her letters to Remo, therefore, sacred letters—and tears them piece by piece into two pieces. That makes many, many pieces when Remo gets home.

When Remo saw the pile of pieces, he cried or almost cried, dear Friedericke. I also cried for the sake of my letters and my sanity. Wilhelm is hand in glove with Mother Luck, a glove of silence. If she is willpower become flesh, then he is weak will become flesh. Yes, yes, he nods at everything, holds her little old hands like a silly old man and carries the hot-water bottle for her. He lets Justi visit secretly, he idolizes Remo, and he ignores me because that's what Mother Luck wants. And pretty soon I won't want this anymore.

———

Eva, in contrast, isn't ashamed of anything but her virginity. On weekends, when Gorda is sitting in dreary Bunten and Vreni in the dreary mansion in Linzingen, Eva loads up her Volkswagen—she's the only one with a car because her father owns a VW dealership in Bonn—with hiking boots, windbreaker, and binoculars and drives to the mountains to hike through them. Everywhere, like-minded students are hiking about; students who would like to free Eva of her virginity. But she's still observing with her binoculars, looking around at the handsome guys of the land a little longer to make sure the right guy is indeed the right guy.

Sometimes, Gorda would rather hike through the mountains like this, with binoculars and walking stick and virginity instead of lying, with the rat in her heart, in bed with Remo.

Because she had promised her parents to find a job in Lausanne, she answered an ad and went to an interview in an office. "Well, you attend the École de Français Moderne," the friendly older man said in new German, "and you want to work as a secretary for us. Why would you want to do that? My child, you should think about it." Gorda thought about it that instant. "Thank you very much for your advice," she said joyfully. She went to a phone booth in the huge post office at the Place St. François. "You should keep going to university, the man said. An office job wouldn't suit me, it be totally wrong for me, he said. You only do this kind of job if you need to. And I don't need to. After all, the money comes from my grandmother and I rightfully own it."

Mom didn't say anything after that.

In Bunten, Mother Luck's brother was visiting with his wife and his son and the son's bride. But the family is not interested in the bride as a bride in the family. The brother and his son were shouting all night long, and the women were also shouting, just in a more womanly manner. Remo doesn't know either why they are not interested in the bride as a bride in the family. "Her bed sheets must not be befitting the family's social status," Remo said, giggling. Gorda would've loved to exorcise his giggling. "No, I won't come to visit Bunten, not next week and not the week after," she said, at which point he finally stopped giggling. "But you've got to come and visit," he said. "My mother's birthday is in a week, Wilhelm is coming and an old friend of my mother's, Mrs. Teller."

"I just won't come," she said.

So Remo went to Lausanne instead of staying in Bunten for his mother's birthday. "I told her that I needed to go to the library in Zurich. But whether or not she believed it, I don't know either. Could you possibly think I was looking forward to celebrating my mother's birthday with Wilhelm and Mrs. Teller? The only thing that matters is our love."

And the only thing that matters is that I don't want any of this anymore. Yet she did go to Bunten for Volker and Hanne's wedding. Mother Luck looked at the walls with her This-is-not-fair look, Wilhelm held her old little hands as comfort, and Gorda felt drearily clad in gray feathers in her bright yellow chiffon dress, which had been so pretty when she first tried it on in the shop in Oldenburg. Everything turns gray in Bunten, I don't get it, Gorda thinks and smears rouge on her faded lips.

Hanne looks beautiful in her white dress of honor although Remo giggled: "They have to get married."

"Why do they have to get married?" Gorda asked concerned.

"Hanne is four months pregnant."

Aren't there any engagements and weddings here without this miserable "Have-to," Gorda thought angrily, but only inwardly, please, nothing is to be shown outwardly here.

While drinking coffee for breakfast, Remo tells his mother about the wedding reception: "There definitely had to be over a hundred people there. Volker's whole family down to cousins three, four, five times removed." Remo shakes with giggles. "And the cousins of the cousins were there, and only the mother on Hanne's side. Of course, that stands out: one lone mother among a hundred cousins."

Gorda knows that something has to be said at this moment, something she had been meaning to say for a long time. And she says: "We won't ever celebrate our wedding in this manner!"

As if at the push of a button in her head and gut, Mother Luck erupts from her comfortable armchair: "He-won't-ever-marry-you! He-won't-ever-marry-you!" She keeps yelling in Swiss German and in a consistent rhythm as though she were drumming an eternal truth into Gorda and her unruly son. At the same time, with her hands flailing in defense, she knocks over a huge vase made of white china, its fragments shattering all over the multi-colored Persian rug like snowflakes across a blooming autumn meadow. Gorda expected a reaction but none so honest. Instinctively startled, she starts to pick up the fragments as she would have done at home, a well brought-up daughter, here an ugly Cinderella before the grand ball, she kneels on both knees in the fragments while Mother Luck keeps yelling: "He-won't-ever-marry-you! He-won't-ever-marry-you!"

We're done with humility, Gorda thinks, carefully places the fragments onto the desk, and looks at Remo with the most devastating of all the Mother-Luck glances. "Say something already," she orders. And as he still doesn't say anything, she openly kicks his left shin with her right foot, underscoring her demand and using surprising force. Kicked in this manner, he finally says: "You've got to accept the fact that she exists, Mother."

"I-don't-have-to-do-a-thing!   I-don't-have-to-do-a-thing!" She yells: "He-won't-ever-marry-you! He-won't-ever-marry-you!" Gorda feels obliged to kick Remo a second time. So he comes alive, the man, whom she has loved for more than three years and whom she now, for the last few minutes perhaps or, at least, but that can't be true, no, no, under no circumstances—the man she loves comes alive as with both hands he grabs an empty wine bottle that stood on the old desk. The bottle comes crashing down on the heavy dark-brown oak, for surely it's got to be oak, and thousand upon thousand shards fly jubilating through the room.

"I've had it up to here!" Remo yells.

"It's all her fault," Mother Luck yells. "Because of her my own son lied to me and betrayed me!"

"Silence! Silence!" Remo yells. And there's not a hint of giggling in his raised voice. As he grabs a second bottle, this time a full one, and threatens with it, Mother Luck finally stops her dreadful shrieking. And so Gorda's eve-of-the-wedding party, with its traditional breaking of glass, didn't take place on a Saturday, as would have been customary, but on a Sunday morning in April of that year.

From now on Remo comes to Lausanne. "You've got to write her," he told Gorda. She said no. "And if I gave you a small watch just like the one your friend Vreni has?"

"No," Gorda said.

"And if I'd come with you to Oldenburg in the summer?"

"No," Gorda said.

"And if I'd gave you a ring? Yes, the plain one, the … well, you know. But I'm not wearing a ring, I can tell you that. And in Bunten you can't wear it either. I need to finish my dissertation first, but that will be soon, I promise, definitely. In a couple of months. I'll sign up for my exams. My dissertation advisor highly praised the first part. It just flowed out of me. So it's become clear that the extended preparations paid off."

And so, Gorda wrote a letter: Dear Madam, please accept my sincere apologies for … and got a delicate golden ring in return, one that isn't really a ring but a protective band.

This summer, Gorda visits Bunten only one more time: for Remo's birthday. She takes a bouquet of Mother Luck's favorite flowers to her, red and white carnations, which Gorda hates. Mother Luck accepts them with the smile of embittered desperation. She knows that she has lost her son in this battle, Gorda thinks and, contentedly, feels the ring in the pocket of her blazer. Some of my feathers are green now, even though no one has noticed. Yet everything else stays in hues of gray.

View from the hills above Bunten towards the south

Mother Luck and Wilhelm speak Middle Ages, and Remo
and Gorda secretly whisper modern times. As often as she can,
Gorda disappears in the room with the blue flower design,
which is a protective band although the enemy is lurking under
the bed, in the desk drawer, and in the linen closet.

—————

"Vreni did promise her parents not to see Mathias anymore,
Friedericke. But the promise was forced, making it null and
void, so of course she kept meeting with him. For example,
she went with him to the music festival in Linzingen. And by
peculiar coincidence, the TV camera caught a glimpse of their
faces. You know: cut to the blissfully amazed audience, and there
they were blissfully amazed: Vreni's and Mathias's faces next to
each other on the TV screens in the living rooms of Vreni's
brothers and sisters, of whom she has many, all of Linzingen
is thoroughly Catholic. They were thoughtful enough to let
their parents know. And the parents exiled her to a university
in Australia for the time being. And who knows to where else
if that country proves to be useless against love. Romeo and
Juliet are not dead but live in Linzingen in a mansion and with
a father who adores female dancers too much.

—————

Gorda and Remo's engagement was celebrated in the Deer Inn in Bunten on Lake Thun on September 29th of the same year. Gorda's parents had picked the place, Remo, the restaurant. Remo seemed depressed. And soon someone will start talking about a forced engagement. But that's all the same to me.